Gracie Hill's first n‌‌‌‌‌‌‌‌‌‌‌
romance story that ‌‌‌‌‌‌‌‌‌‌‌‌‌‌‌‌‌‌‌‌‌‌‌‌ y‌‌‌ ‌‌‌‌‌‌‌ ‌‌‌‌ ‌‌‌ ‌‌‌‌‌ ‌‌‌‌‌‌‌
with her colorful characters. Below are a couple of the book's reviews:

In Where The Brothers At? first-time author Gracie Hill brings a fresh, hear-me-roar voice to today's single African-American woman. Through her protagonist Darcel, Hill takes the reader on one Black woman's personal journey for love and fulfillment that resonates by tackling head-on hot-button issues such as interracial relationships, pre-marital sex and adoption. In much the way that Terry McMillan's Stella got her groove back, Hill's Darcel finds where the brothers at. You'll laugh, you'll cry and you'll cheer for her to the heart-warming end.

-Randy Richardson, president of
Chicago Writers Association

Where the Brothers At? is a cleverly crafted romance novel with colorful characters, an engaging story line, and social commentary immensely relevant to today's dating and relationship scene. It's a provocative page-turner!

-Jennifer Brown Banks
Columnist at Online Dating Magazine, editor and author

To: Jon Goldsmith.

Sorrows
OF THE HEART

Live
Your
Dreams.

Sorrows OF THE HEART

Gracie HILL

Wasteland Press
Shelbyville, KY USA
www.wastelandpress.net

Sorrows of the Heart
by Gracie Hill

Copyright © 2009 Gracie Hill
ALL RIGHTS RESERVED

Second Printing – September 2009
ISBN: 978-1-60047-300-5

NO PART OF THIS BOOK MAY BE REPRODUCED IN
ANY FORM, BY PHOTOCOPYING OR BY ANY
ELECTRONIC OR MECHANICAL MEANS, INCLUDING
INFORMATION STORAGE OR RETRIEVAL SYSTEMS,
WITHOUT PERMISSION IN WRITING FROM THE
COPYRIGHT OWNER/AUTHOR.

Printed in the USA

To my children

Deveron, Tretara, Martin-Nique, Tarara, Mason,
Frederick and Carrie

Live a life that lives on, even after you're gone!

I love you!

To my wonderful husband, Brian K. Hill, who is amazingly
supportive and my biggest fan, you encourage me and you
even do more promoting of my books than I do. Your input
and contribution to this book helped to mold the end
product. Thank you Sweetheart!

I love you!

Read excerpts of other upcoming titles at

www.graciehill.com

Acknowledgements

I thank the Lord for all his many blessings great and small and for allowing me to live my dreams.

To my sister, Machelle Wood - You are extremely talented. Thank you for all the work you do on my website and the marketing efforts that you pour yourself over in order to help me promote my books. I love you!

To Alma Bass, my editor and friend - You are such an awesome woman of God. You have impacted my life from the first day that I met you and you continue to do so. Your labor invested in this book is greatly appreciated.

Thank you so very much to all of you who buy my books. Your support is necessary and more appreciated than you can know. I pray that God will richly bless your life.

Gracie Hill

Chapter 1

Being in prison is like attending your own funeral. The difference is, you get to see who comes to pay their last respects. What I mean is, you serve your time alone with your three stonewalls and a doorway of impenetrable iron bars. You have no friends, just co-conspirators, everybody struggling to live another day. The conspiracy unfolds everyday in the chow line, on the yard, in the shower and in your sleep as every eye and hand awaits an opportunity to make the breath you breathe your last.

You may have a few loved ones, maybe even a friend or two on the outside, who write you and hopefully put a little money on your books. Those will be the few that sit on the front pew dressed in black to view your body lying in the casket.

But, by the time the pastor gives the eulogy and the service comes to an end, you'll see just how few people really do show up to pay their last respects. I'm living it right now, front and center. I watched the pallbearers bring in my body. When it was all over only one person stood at the gravesite as my cold steel black casket was lowered into the ground. My girl Somara stood there alone. Her eyes filled with tears and her heart filled with love, for me. She was the only person that attended my funeral. That is a cold, hard, hurtful truth. But so it is!

My father walked out on us when my brother, Maurice, and I were both very young. My mother died many years ago leaving us with no other close family, at least any that I knew about. That's why I sit here in this prison cell angry with myself for the choices I made which put me here and left Somara there all alone.

The jury found me guilty of manufacturing and trafficking narcotics with the intent to sell. The judge looked at me with an ice-cold stare that chilled my blood. I knew then that he would be giving me the maximum sentence. "I sentence you to twenty years, two hundred and forty months, to be served in a federal penitentiary." The judge pronounced the sentence with no emotion. Twenty years! The sound of it pierced my ears and it was as if time stood still from that moment to this one.

Before that sentence I had a life, a beautiful home, more than one, and more money than I could spend. More importantly, I had a woman that not only loved me but also adored me! Let me tell you about the life that I lived and the slow death steps, which led me to the jail cell funeral I'm living right now.

My mother, Vera, named me Malcolm because she said she wanted me to stand for something and she needed me to believe that I was destined for great things. She was a strong woman that raised both of her sons by herself. Our father left when my little brother, Maurice, was two years old. I remember the day he walked out on us. But not before he slapped my mother as hard as he could. They were arguing about money, the thing that causes the demise of so many relationships and lives. I heard my father tell my mother, "I never wanted any little bastard kids. I told you that."

I was only six years old. But it hurt me to hear the words he said to her. Even though, at the time, I didn't know what the words meant. But I knew enough to know he was talking about Maurice and me. I never forgot those cruel words that hurt me and crushed my mother and made her cry. Even now the tears my mother shed that day, and every day after, have felt like nails in my coffin.

I never saw my father again. My brother and I grew up watching our mother work and worry herself endlessly. She worked a lot so that Maurice and I could have the things we needed. She tried really hard to make up for our father not being with us. But a mother can not be a father. Not to a man-child. I can't think of a day she just didn't go to work. She never called in sick or left work early. Even when she was sick, she went to work.

My mother worked third-shift. She was determined to be the one to send us off to school and be there for us after school with fresh baked cookies and milk. Looking back, it appears there was no reason for me to choose the destructive pathway in life which led me right here to this temporary dead end. I'm blessed because, for me, it is temporary. Some people never leave!

School came easy to me and I got very good grades. I didn't have to do a lot of studying. Not even for the harder classes like Algebra or Trigonometry. I was glad because that meant I had enough free time to get a job at a neighborhood grocery store, working after school and on the weekends. I didn't make a lot of money. But I made enough to keep spending money in my brother's pocket and decent kicks on his feet, so he would feel good about himself.

By the time I was nineteen, things began to look up for us. Unfortunately, that didn't last long. I had gotten a full ride scholarship to Chicago State University. It was my freshman year, I had a plan and I meant to work it. My brother Maurice was fifteen and a freshman in High School. We both promised Mama we would stay focused and do our best in school. My mother was beyond proud of her boys. She was determined we would both finish college with a degree and have solid careers.

She also meant for us to give back to our community. So whatever career path we chose, she had instilled in our minds that nobody makes it on their own. We knew we would have to do something to mentor some young brothers along the way.

My mother had done a good job of raising us on her own. She kept us together, out of trouble, and in school. Mama gave us a desire to make it out of the projects while not forgetting where we came from. She was a strong woman and the glue that held our family together. Maurice and I were about to be hit with that as a cold hard reality. This is where my story gets twisted!

In the projects where we lived, gunfire and the piercing sound of police sirens were almost as common as an alarm clock going off every morning. So when I heard multiple gunfire, it didn't move me from my bed. Besides, the safest place to be when bullets were flying sure wasn't looking out of a window trying to see what was going on. My mother always told us, "A bullet doesn't have anybody's name on it. It doesn't care who it claims." It took the pounding on our apartment door to shake me from my bed. For a few seconds my thoughts were foggy. Then I remembered that my mother was at work and Maurice had spent the night at his best friends house. So I thought to myself who could be pounding on the door like that?

When I opened the door, Janice, the young woman who lived in the next apartment, was standing in front of me. Her face was drenched in tears. "Malcolm, your mother has been shot." Those words paralyzed me for a few seconds. I couldn't move. I couldn't even feel my body. I didn't know if I was still alive. Janice grabbed my shoulders and shook me. "Malcolm, she's down stairs in the front of the building." Janice took my hand and pulled me out of the doorway. Then my heart started to beat again and I felt my feet moving as I ran down the stairs to the front of the apartment building.

I stepped in my mother's blood as I took the last two steps before I knelt down beside her body. I could feel and hear the thick red blood that oozed from underneath my shoes. I took my mother's hand as I looked into her eyes because I thought she would be scared. I didn't see any fear. Concern filled her eyes. Concern for the two sons she knew she was about to leave behind. Her body was covered with blood. I couldn't even tell where she had been shot. My tears fell down onto her bloody body. I felt my mother's hand cradle my right cheek. She never said a word, but her last breath and the gentle touch of her hand on my face, told me that she loved my brother and me and we were to love each other to life.

That was a phrase my mother would always say to us whenever my brother and I argued. I can hear her voice now saying, "You're brothers! You both have the same life sustaining blood coursing through your veins. One day, you'll only have each other because mama won't be here with you always baby. So each of you will need to be your brother's keeper. Be good to each other, take care of each other, and love each other to life."

Man those words became the driving force behind my commitment to take care of my brother at all costs.

Chapter 2

My first year of college went by quickly. I kept my grade point average between a 3.75 and 4.0, which meant there was no danger of losing my financial aide. But I was in danger of losing everything else. My mother had been dead for almost a year. Her life insurance money was about to run out. I had to do something and I didn't have a long time to figure out what that something needed to be.

My boy Jay, I grew up with him, was always down with the streets. Jay never asked me, tempted me, or in any way tried to get me involved in the street game. He would tell me on a regular basis, "Man, you too smart for the streets. The street game is for brothers with no other options." My self-image always stood up straight whenever he said that to me. But the weight of life's reality was bearing down on me hard. I would have to bend over to carry the load. I considered all of my options and made a decision I felt it took a man to make. I made a phone call I knew that I would regret.

"Jay, what's up man? This is Malcolm."

"What's up School Boy?"

"Not much Jay, just trying to make it man. But I do need to holla at you about something whenever you can talk."

"No problem School Boy. Meet me at the spot in thirty minutes."

The moment I hung up the phone, regret tore through my stomach and my soul. So I kept my mind focused on the fact that I had to keep my brother in school, out of jail, and out of an early grave. It didn't take long before I was standing face to face with a revolving door that would prove to be more than difficult to stop.

When I turned the corner at 63rd Street, I saw Jay's black Escalade sitting up on twenties and dressed down in chrome from bumper to bumper. When I reached for the door handle, I heard the locks release. I stepped up into the vehicle and sat down on leather seats so soft I felt like I was sitting on a pillow top mattress. The locks on the doors clamped down securing us in the vehicle. The second the prison cell door closed behind me, I thought back to the locks on Jay's ride sounding off loudly in my ear. That had actually been the day my prison sentence began.

"School Boy, you looking good man. How you living?"

"I'm living man, barely but I'm living."

"What's going on baby?"

"Jay, man, you always told me I was too smart for the streets. Right now, I got to be a man in the streets. My mother has been gone almost a year now. I'm in college and Maurice is a sophomore in high school. That's where I need his head to be, in school. Not sweat'n some going nowhere job, or worse, following in behind some wannabe gang bangers."

"I got to see my brother with a degree in his hand, some options in front of him, and we've got to get out of the projects. Ida B Wells housing projects won't claim his life the way it did my mother's. It cost to live and I know that I might have to pay to play. But that's a risk I'm going to have to take."

"Malcolm, I know you not asking me to deal you a hand."

"Jay, I'm out of options. You said the game is for brothers with no other options. As far as I know, you're the coldest in the dope game. I need you to let me sit in on a hand or two."

"You sure about that, School Boy?"

"My circumstances make me sure."

"Alright man, I got you."

Jay did what I asked him to do, but he more than had my back every step of the way. He brought me in the game slowly. I started out way behind the scenes; running errands for Jay, delivering messages and dropping off small-unknown packages to where I was told to take them.

Then I moved up to running large quantities of drugs to other drug dealers that Jay supplied. I never expected to be anywhere near gunfire or blood. I guess I wasn't too realistic. Bae-Bae, Drae and I went to a hotel to meet up with some buyers from Indianapolis. They wanted to buy two Kilos of cocaine. Jay sent three of us because it was a large amount of dope and some heavy cash that was suppose to change hands.

The deal turned into a stick up. Once they had inspected the dope, we made sure they had the cash. But as the exchange was about to take place, old boy from Indianapolis put a gun to Drae's head as he yelled, "I know you fools ain't willing to die for somebody else's money."

Drae was the kind of brother that was always ready to take every confrontation to the battlefield. As soon as he said, "Hell naw, we ain't dying for somebody else's money. But you ain't just gonna put a gun to my head and turn around and walk away either," he pushed old boy and reached for the gun he had in his back.

Before Drae could get to his piece, old boy pulled the trigger on his nine-millimeter. Bae-Bae shot out the light in the ceiling. I hit the floor. Gunfire was going off all around me. The room was lit up with nine-millimeter bullets looking for a fatal target.

For months after that I walked around in a daze. I don't know how I concentrated on anything, because sleep for me was almost impossible. When I did fall asleep, I could see the gun being placed at Drae's head and I could feel the impact of his blood shoot out of his head onto my face.

It could have just as easily been my blood on him. I could have been the one falling dead on the floor. I thought I was tough before I saw that brother get shot while standing right next to me. Three of us walked into that hotel room. I was the only one of us that walked out. I should say, "ran out." Drae got killed; Bae-Bae was beaten almost to death. He stayed in a comma for three months. If it hadn't been for him shooting out that light, I'm sure that day would have been my day to die. Somehow I made it through that and a few other stupid things that happened over the next few years.

Time went by quickly. I guess between finishing college with an MBA and dealing drugs, I didn't have much time to think about the pages turning on the calendar. It felt good to see Mama's dream come true for me. I took the walk of honor and got my degree placed in my hand.

The only thing that was missing that day was my mama flashing that big prideful grin she wore every time Maurice and I did something that she expected of us. She would hug us so tight we could hardly breath. Her voice saying, "Baby, Mama so proud of you. You be a good man and always do what you know is right," I could almost hear her voice in my ear when I walked across the stage.

Maurice wasn't too far behind me. He was close to finishing school. Maurice was determined to be a defense attorney. I know Mama was in heaven shouting up a storm over that decision. I had no doubt in my mind that Maurice would do exactly what Mama expected of both of us.

A different mission would drive the next few years for me. I wouldn't just be dealing drugs on the side. I would be dealing drugs up close and personal on a large scale. I wouldn't be working for Jay anymore. I would be working for myself.

The young man my mama had known me to be was definitely about to change. For that reason, I figured I needed to have a conversation with my mother before I wasn't recognizable. I went to her gravesite in Oakwood cemetery.

I always thought it was a little weird for people to talk to the dead in a cemetery, looking down at a headstone with the name of their loved one carved in it. Yet there I was and for some reason, the fact that I was there to talk to my mother didn't seem weird at all.

It took me almost an hour to find my mother's headstone. It had been a few years since I put flowers on her gravesite. The closer I got to it, the heavier the tears welling up in my eyes felt. I was surprised that the cold cruel winter air that belonged to the Windy City wasn't discouraging me from my search. I swallowed hard as I looked at her name carved in the cold rock hard headstone. *Vera Johnson – A mother that loved us past her heart.* I could almost hear her voice saying those very words. When we were little and she put us to bed at night, she would tell us that she loved us past her heart.

Although it was the first time I visited her gravesite to talk and not just leave flowers, I didn't struggle for the words to say to her.

"I know you probably didn't expect to hear my voice. I know I didn't expect to be talking. But I needed you to know that I'm about to step a little further away from the man you raised me to be. I've done some things over the last few years that I am not proud of. People are quick to say, "I didn't have a choice," when they do something wrong and they're ashamed of it. I won't say I didn't have a choice, but I made the choice that I felt I could make work at the time."

"Mama, I haven't killed anybody. I'm not strung out on drugs, and I don't have a child somewhere that I'm not taking care of. But I am about to walk a little further down a pathway you wouldn't approve of. I promise the journey will be a temporary one. Keep watching over me because I need to always feel your love. Mama, know that I love you!"

I walked away from my mama that day and walked further into a life of crime that set the framework for the story that I'm telling you now.

Chapter 3

When I first got in the game, folks called me School Boy. But the ladies called me "Chicago Slick." Now a brother wasn't half stepping at all. I dressed cold and you could smell me coming a block away. I didn't mind spending money on designer colognes because you don't have to use a lot of it to smell good. Cologne sprayed on a shirt lingered for a week even after I took it off. My well-groomed black mustache and goa-tee complimented my medium brown smooth complexion. Working out and bulking up my biceps, triceps and pecks was a must on a regular basis. I was a thick muscular brother.

I could wear the hell out of a suit and I had occasion to wear them daily since I had started my own consulting company. At least that was the nine to five cover that I had quite successfully learned to portray. The business made pretty good money too. My office in Dearborn Park wasn't anything too flashy that would draw unwanted attention. The small suite, with two offices and a reception area, provided the modest visual I wanted, along with a nice view of the Chicago lakefront.

My office was furnished with some stylish cherry wood furniture: a computer credenza, an executive style desk, palladium hutch and lateral filing cabinet. The chair I sat in and ruled what I felt to be my empire was a high back, supreme comfort, burgundy leather chair that perfectly matched my desk. The custom made chair offered a full back and neck massage or a lower lumbar massage. You know, it just depended on the kind of day I was having. I learned a little bit about style and choosing furniture. Money will do that for you. The practice would come in handy for the house I would buy later down the road.

There were several very nice pieces of Black art hanging on the walls. I had met a few artists in college. They displayed some of their pieces in my office, which got some exposure for their work and even sold some of it. I was also able to get the owner of the building to agree to let them display some of the their art in other areas of the building. The location and decor definitely made the statement that my small consultant firm was thriving.

I was on the rise. A lot of years had past and I had just turned thirty-two. A few days later, to my surprise, I met the woman that made me love her.

The first time I laid eyes on Somara Hughes was in downtown Chicago. I was getting out of a taxi at the corner of Washington and State Street. She was running across the street to grab the taxi I was getting out of. The sleek ruby red dress she wore lay closely against her body as the wind blew. I held the taxi door for her. She smiled at me and said, "Thank you." Her soft hand brushed against mine while she reached for the top of the door to brace herself. I watched her petite, firm, frame slide into the seat. The smell of her perfume lingered behind and wouldn't let me forget her. I couldn't even speak as she got into the taxi. I wanted to. I just couldn't believe I was looking at such a lusciously beautiful woman that I would never see again.

A month later I did see her again, downtown, going into a little corner restaurant. I had an appointment I was already twenty minutes late for. I rescheduled it because I couldn't pass up the chance to try to meet her, the red dress beauty.

I went into the restaurant and I saw her almost immediately. She was sitting alone at a table, in the corner, next to a glass wall aquarium filled with exotic fish. I asked the maitre d' to seat me near her. She was eating a salad and drinking a glass of wine. I ordered a salad as well and sat hoping that she would look up and our eyes would meet. That would give us an opportunity to speak to each other. A brother just needed a smooth way to get her attention.

She was almost finished with her salad. It didn't appear that she had ordered anything else. I was running out of time. I decided to take a chance. As I approached her table, she looked up and our eyes met. I figured I had one chance and I had better be genuine and not try to shoot game at her. She didn't look like the type of woman to be played with.

I smiled at her. When I reached her table my words came out calm and sincere. "I apologize for the intrusion. I've been sitting at my table hoping that you would look up at me, our eyes would meet and we could say hello. That didn't happen which is why I'm standing here interrupting your dinner. Maybe you don't remember me. I held a taxi for you about a month ago at the corner of Washington and State Street. I was getting out of the taxi and you were running across the street trying to get the driver's attention."

"You got my attention in the red dress you were wearing that day. I've thought of you often since then. I was sure that I would never see you again. But there you were walking into this restaurant. I had to come in behind you and hope there would be a chance for us to meet. Long hello ha? Sorry about that."

"Actually, I wondered if you were going to come over and say anything to me. Perhaps I should say that I was hoping you were going to come over and say something to me. I remember you holding the taxi that day. Your smile and the smell of the cologne you were wearing didn't leave my mind too quickly. I think you have on the same cologne today. May I ask what it is that you're wearing?"

"Boucheron! It's one that I wear often. It's a good thing I decided to wear it today."

"Would you like to join me?"

"Yes, I would. Thank you! I'm Malcolm D. Johnson."

"My name is Somara Hughes. What's the D for, Malcolm?"

"The D is for my determination to get to know you." I couldn't help but laugh at myself for saying something so lame. She laughed with me. I told her the D was really for Darryl. That evening began a whirlwind romance for us. We grew close quickly.

The moment she walked into my life, Somara had a maturing impact on me. She was a couple of years older than me. I was a brother that slid in and out from between the sheets with women on a dangerous frequency. Somara was very explicit when she laid down the law about what she would and wouldn't accept. The tone in her voice was probably the most stern I had ever heard her use. That was the beginning of our monogamist relationship.

We had been dating for about two months when I took her out to dinner at the Signature Room. One of the several women that I dated regularly walked up to the dinner table where we were sitting. She asked Somara who she was and why was she with her man? Somara handled herself like a lady. She smiled as she stood and turned to me and said in a calm voice, "I believe those questions would be better answered by you." As she looked at the woman straight in her eyes, she said to me, "If you don't handle this, I will." Then with the same calm voice she said, "Excuse me while I go to the ladies room."

She had enough class and self-control to leave the table and give me time to deal with the uncouth behavior of Miss Thang who had rudely interrupted our dinner. As Somara returned to the table, I remember thinking, "This woman isn't just beautiful, she's gorgeous." Even though I'm 6 feet tall, my preference in a woman has always been for the short to medium height, petite, bright skin sistahs. She ranked top in all those categories. Her graceful stride, the way her dress hugged her small waist, the smooth sway of the flared bottom of her black, form fitting, knit dress whisking back and forth said sexy. But those soft, grayish, green eyes that could look at you and yet right through you, held the pulse of my heart.

Moments after she reached the table and sat that fine sexy body down next to me, and smiled at me sweetly, her usual soft voice took on a stern tone, and rang out clearly. "If you want me, then it will have to be only me because I don't share. You men meet a good woman who is actually a treasure and you have the audacity to think you can disrespect her with your see through lies, your player, player games, a seductive smile, and a kiss that you think will disarm her brain, and disrobe her body at the same time. Think again brother, it ain't happening. Treat me with some respect and consideration, know the meaning of the word monogamy, and be committed to it, and you might have a chance with me."

The firm words that flowed from her mouth hit me like bricks. Somara meant every word she said. The stern, unyielding look in her eyes told me she was not willing to accept any of the slick lies I was so skillful at telling or any of the games I usually ran on the women.

I wanted this woman and what she thought of me mattered. No woman before her pulled at my heartstrings. Somara made me desire one woman and one woman only, her. Our relationship blossomed into the first and only love affair I thought I would know. The love I felt for her was beyond my ability to understand. I wanted her around me all the time. When I was away from her, thoughts of her never left my mind. That was definitely not my style. She was the woman who changed my heart.

Somara brought breath to my life. She made me want to be a better man. She taught me to live and not just exist. She was an only child. I think that's why she loved me hard and I gave her that same hard love in return. Somara was definitely a woman that desired to be with only one man. Her devotion to me made me love her more.

You see the game that I was in required me to know that I could trust her with my life. That kind of trust had to come by way of actions. Before I could trust her with my life I needed to know that I could trust her with my heart. A friend of mine, Winston, was in town visiting his family. We were pretty tight in college. He was a playboy for sure and a nice looking brother that the women seemed to find irresistible. He would do just fine for what I had in mind.

Chapter 4

Winston would be in town for a week. I told him about Somara and that I needed to know if I could trust her. He was quick to agree to help me feel her out. Winston thought there wasn't a woman alive that could resist him. I told him where she worked and I needed his game to be strong because I had to be sure about this woman.

Winston went to the Chicago Art Museum and asked about some specific artwork and its history. The young lady he questioned referred him to Somara, since she was head of the art procurement department. Winston was good. He had created an opportunity to meet Somara. My girl knew her stuff. Winston said she gave him more info than he was able to follow. He smiled at her a lot while she answered his questions. When she was finished, he told her she was a very beautiful woman. He said her only response was "Thank you!"

Winston seemed a little surprised that she wasn't moved at all by the attention he showed her. He went back to the museum the next day and asked to speak to Somara because he had a complaint. Somara met him at the information counter where he was standing. Winston laid out for me the conversation between the two of them like a tape recorder.

"Hello Ms. Hughes. I'm sorry to disturb you, but I want to lodge a complaint."

"Mr. Barnes, right? What's your complaint? I'd be happy to address your concern."

"I'm flattered that you remember my name and I'm sure that you can help me. My complaint is that I met you yesterday but I don't know you. I would very much like the opportunity to get acquainted. I'd like to take you to lunch, if I may?"

"I appreciate your interest. I have to be honest with you. I am very much involved with someone and I treasure what we have together. I won't jeopardize that. Lunch would be inappropriate!"

"It's only lunch. You have to eat don't you?"

"Thank you, Mr. Barnes but I brought my lunch."

"Okay, how about a cup of coffee?"

"I need to get back to my office. Enjoy your afternoon."

"Forgive my intrusion Ms. Hughes. Have a good day."

Winston sounded confident that Somara couldn't be moved from her statement of fidelity. I wasn't as easily convinced. I told Winston he needed to turn up the heat a little. Give Somara something to think about. We discussed it and quickly came up with a plan of action. The details of our conversation still stand out in my mind.

"How hot do you want the flames Malcolm?"

"Man, don't cross the line! I'm just saying stir up her curiosity about what might be behind door number two. I'll send her some orchids. She loves those. I'm sure she'll wonder why you chose orchids and not roses. That should be a simple enough attention grabber."

"Okay, have the flowers delivered by one o'clock. I've got a couple of things to do in the morning. I can stop by to see her in the early afternoon."

"All right Winston, give me a call at my office after you've seen Somara."

"Man, even I've never gone to this extreme to see where I stood with a woman."

"Yeah, you've never given a woman your heart either. You've just always taken theirs and each of them had to take a number and stand in line for your time and attention. I love this woman and she has my heart!"

"I feel you brother. I'll talk to you tomorrow."

I thought about our conversation, hoping that I wasn't setting myself up to be hurt. I sat in my office for the next hour playing two scenarios over and over in my mind. Somara would not be moved by all of Winston's charm, flattering words, and diligent efforts to gain her interest. If she didn't, that meant I wouldn't have been able to help myself from falling more and more in love with her. Even though I wanted to love her like that, I was afraid to love someone so completely. With that type of love came another level of trust. Which meant I would let my guard down and I would be vulnerable in my heart and with my life. The game I was in vulnerability was a dangerous card to play.

The second scenario definitely had a different flavor. If Somara flinched in her heart in anyway like she remotely was interested in Winston, I would have to cut that sistah out of my life quick and hard. It would hurt, and for sure, it would be a hard thing to do. But I had decided that I would have to chalk it up to a lesson learned in trust that didn't cost me my life.

My mind was caught up in how that would all play out. I was glad to see Maurice's number calling my cell phone. I needed to get back to reality.

"What's up little brother?"

"Man, I'm 28 years old and you still calling me that."

"You'll always be my little brother and nothing can change that. Now what's going on with you?"

"Not much Malcom. Just wanted you to know I landed that job with Wilcox & Williams Law Firm," Maurice said to me with a teasing tone in his voice.

"Maurice man, I'm proud of you is a serious understatement. You've done everything I've asked you to do. You stayed focused on school. You lived and breathed those law books.

You stayed away from drugs, gangs, and you called me when you needed me, even if it was just to talk. You stayed on the Dean's list pulling down nothing but straight A's. I knew this day would come. Wilcox & Williams, one of the biggest law firms in Atlanta. That's what I'm talking about. My little brother doing it!"

"Man please, you made all that possible. Not me! I would still be in the projects dodging bullets; trying to keep turning down the drug dealers on every corner that were busy trying to get me to either buy some dope or sell some dope. That's why I gave you my law degree to hang next to your MBA. When Mama died, you stepped in her shoes and you never missed a step. What ever I needed, you made sure I had it. I'm never going to forget that, Man. No matter what you do in this life, I love you and I'll always have your back."

"My brother's keeper, remember? I couldn't do anything else."

"Thanks man, much love! Now, what's up with Somara with her fine self?"

"Yeah, the sistah is fine, ha? She's doing well! We're doing well! Maurice, I'm just trying to keep my feet on the ground.

She's moving me into some seriously uncharted emotional waters."

"Relax and enjoy Malcolm. You deserve it."

"Thanks man! Let's do dinner next week, you, Somara and me. We've got to celebrate this new job of yours."

"Sounds like a plan. I'll call you this weekend and we'll work out the when and where."

"Keep your head up little brother."

That was pretty much how the conversation went between Maurice and me. I was happy for my little brother. He had done better than good. Some times even now I can hear his crazy laugh and the joy in his voice while he's telling me about moving to Atlanta for his new job. I reach out to hug him and let him know how proud of him I am. Then I wake up and looking at the bars that keep me in my cell remove all doubt. I can't touch him because it was a dream. Some times yesterday seems so much apart of today.

After hearing the news about Maurice's new job, I wondered what it would be like to watch him in the courtroom defending someone. I wasn't looking forward to him leaving

Chicago. Between Maurice and Somara, I had a lot on my mind. Even Denise, the young woman who worked as my secretary, noticed the difference in my demeanor. She was a pretty young woman in her late twenties and a single mom with two kids. Her no good baby daddy didn't pay child support and refused to help her take care of his sons.

My heart was soft when it came to her because she was young enough to be my adult little sister. The worry and stress of struggling to take care of her children was worn clearly on her face daily. Her pain made me think of my mother and the struggle she endured being in the same position. The right thing to do was for me to help her. I paid her very well to work full time in my office. It felt good to be able to help her and see the stress in her life, at least financially, ease up.

It was a part of that giving back thing my mother had instilled in Maurice and me. I also tried to be a positive role model in her boy's lives. They were both good kids. I took them out at least once a month. We would go shopping first and pick up anything they needed clothes wise and a couple of toys or new games for their electronic gaming system.

I made a deal with them. As long as they got A's and B's in school, I would buy each of them at least two new games for their system every month. Plus, I'd take them to the museum, a movie, the zoo or anywhere fun. Men need to reach out and have an impact in some young boys life that otherwise may not have a male influence. I'm confident that will keep some of them out of the gangs, out of trouble, and definitely out of prison. That's not a new concept though. We all know it takes a village. But there aren't enough of us brothers that are willing to invest the time and energy. That needs to change.

Somara supported me in my commitment to Denise's boys. She never once asked me why I did it or if I had been involved with Denise at one time and the boys were mine and I didn't want to admit it. She believed that I just wanted to help and she never stood in the way of that. Her support was just another reason why I loved her and I had to know how deep her love ran for me.

Winston went back to see Somara the next day shortly before the white orchids were scheduled to be delivered to her. He said he made sure he was in her view but did not make eye-to-eye contact with her. He wanted to see if she would approach him first. Winston spent an hour waiting to see if Somara would initiate any contact with him. She did not.

So he left just before the orchids were delivered. I dictated the card to the florist. I wanted the words on the card to be brief but impactful.

Ms. Hughes,

Orchids are not average flowers. Nor is your beauty or the way you make me feel nervous in your presence. If I never get to know you, you will truly be a treasure lost to me.

Sincerely,
Winston

Winston went back to the museum about an hour later. He told me when Somara saw him she initiated a brief conversation. Winston gave me all the details.

"Somara called out to me as she walked across the floor with a stack of papers in her hand. I could smell her perfume before she was actually standing in front of me. She shook my hand very casually as she started talking to me."

"Thank you for the absolutely gorgeous orchids that you sent me earlier this afternoon. They're my favorite. Most men would have sent roses. Why orchids?"

"Roses just didn't seem special enough. From the moment that I met you, I've been totally engulfed with the desire to get to know you. I've tried to put you out of my mind. No woman has ever grabbed my attention the way you have without even trying."

"Mr. Barnes, I am very flattered by your interest in me. Again, the flowers are gorgeous. But I'm not starving for attention. Malcolm showers me with love and attention on a consistent basis. He's the special man in my life. He has filled my heart and my life with everything that I need from a man. I'm very happy."

"I know some women would jump at the chance to see if the grass is greener on the other side. But the grass that I'm standing on feels like a bed of roses. So, I'm going to stay just exactly where I am. If you'll wait a few minutes, I'll get the orchids that you had delivered. I would have refused the delivery, but I wasn't in my office. Someone else accepted the flowers for me."

"Please keep the flowers. I'm impressed by your loyalty to this Malcolm. I can only hope that I will meet a gorgeous woman who will be as faithful to me. I think you are precious and a caliber of woman most men are not fortunate enough to know. Malcolm is truly a lucky man."

At least that was how Winston told me the conversation between the two of them went. But I also knew that Winston liked the women and my woman was finer than most. I needed to be sure he wasn't playing me either. How did I know Somara didn't agree to go out with him and he just told me what I wanted to hear? I went home that evening thinking about how I could have peace about what might or might not be going on with Winston and Somara.

My mind was still wrapped around Somara and the question of infidelity when I went to sleep that night. I woke up at three in the morning drenched in a cold sweat and mad as hell. I woke up out of my dream just before I could see if Somara got into the black limousine that Winston sent to take her to the airport. She had agreed to spend a weekend with him in Punta Cana, an island in the Dominican Republic. That dream gave me an idea for the last test that Somara would have to pass. I would wait for at least a week. Then I would give her the final exam.

Somara did get points for telling me about Winston coming on to her. I wondered if she would keep it from me and justify herself by thinking she turned down each of his advances. So there was no reason for her to tell me. But she told me what happened the first day they met and about the following attempts he made to come on to her. I asked for details. She gave me the same story that Winston had laid out for me. I accepted that temporarily and took solace in what seemed to be a victory for that moment.

Chapter 5

A week seemed to pass by as slow as Christmas took to come once a year. I stayed busy servicing the clients my consultant firm had on the books and pulling money in the back door with the dope game. My empire set up was slick and clean. I had three rules that I never broke. I was never involved in any transactions physically. I kept my money and my dope in separate locations and I trusted no one.

The only man in the game I did trust was Jay and he was dead. Jay was killed in a car jacking. I guess I could have been shot in the head and left on the side of the street too. I had just gotten out of his hummer with him fifteen minutes before it happened. A few weeks later, a guy I knew as Money asked me for a job. I had been acquainted with him for several years. Our paths crossed originally when we were both working for Jay.

Jay called him his Money making line backer. Money definitely had the body of a line backer. He was tall with broad shoulders, muscles bulging from everywhere, and arms that looked like they could crush a two-ton truck with just two strong hits. His size didn't seem to scare the women since he had plenty of them who were willing to give him their time. After he started working for me he became my major front man. Nobody came to me about anything unless they had gone through him first and he knew everything was on the up and up. But you better believe I still did my own checking too. I didn't trust Money, just like I didn't trust anybody else. Though Money did prove to be very valuable to my setup, at least for a while.

Once a week it was straight payday`for me. My boys brought my money to me at our safe house. There the money was counted and my numbers guy documented all the week's transactions and dollar totals into an elaborate accounting system that he created for me. His system would allow me to check and cross check any money, delivery, dope or payouts with just a couple of keystrokes on my laptop. But I was about to take a break from all of that, at least for a couple of days.

Somara and I spent the weekend together. I enjoyed every minute I was with her. She had a way of making me let go of my stress and any issues that caused me concern. My thoughts about her ability to be faithful didn't weigh on my heart at all that weekend. Somara showered me with attention the entire time we were together. I had no reason to think about doubting her for even a moment.

Too bad the sobering reality of Monday washed over me with the ringing of my alarm clock at seven a.m. The first thing I thought about when my eyes opened up was the final test I would put to Somara. I needed to know how it would all end up. Though I wasn't all together sure that I wanted to know the end results. At least I wished that it wasn't necessary.

I got up and moved through my morning as usual. I watched the news, lifted weights, had a cup of coffee, showered, dressed, and was in my office by nine thirty. I was determined to have a viable means of support that was legal. I didn't want the Fed's taking everything I owned because I couldn't show a legal means of support that would allow me to afford the things that I had. I also didn't plan on being in the dope game until I got caught. That was one-thing brothers seemed to always do wrong. You can't make that type of serious hustle a career. You got to have an exit plan.

Make your money, get in a good place financially, set yourself up to go legal, and get out of the game. Because one day when you've made the mistake of feeling comfortable and untouchable, the door gets kicked in, the Fed's are all over you, and you're going down. If not that, the fatal bullet that you had been lucky enough to dodge finds you anyway. I was too smart to end up in either position. Yeah, right! Every brother selling drugs probably said the same thing, all the way to the prison gates.

The first call I made when I got to my office was to a limousine service. I ordered a Mercedes limousine to arrive at Somara's job by five o'clock in the evening. She usually left work at five thirty. Just in case she left a little earlier, the limousine would already be there. The driver was given a picture of Somara and a description of her car. He was instructed to give her a hand written note, which I had one of my boys write for me. The note was soft spoken but direct and written as if it came from Winston.

Ms. Hughes,

Have dinner with me please. I made a reservation at Riva's on the lake for six thirty. I just want to talk. I promise if you just hear me out, I won't bother you again. Please give me a chance. I don't want to have any regrets when I look back over my life. So I had to try one more time to talk to you. I look forward to seeing you at dinner. If not, I hope that your

life is full and happy. You Somara, I believe to be a real
treasure!
Winston

My heart was in the note. It just had Winston's name on it.
Somara was a treasure. That was why I took the chance of
following her into a downtown restaurant when I saw her
again for the second time. I didn't want to have any regrets. I
took a chance then that I've never regretted. The limousine
driver was directed to call my cell phone and let me know if
Somara accepted the limousine ride or not. It was early yet. I
would have to wait the whole day to find out what side of my
heart Somara would end up on.

I had two appointments scheduled for the day. My morning
appointment would take the most time and energy by far. My
client was an entrepreneur who really should have considered
if she had what it takes to run a business and not just start one
because she had enough money to open the doors. A lot of
entrepreneurs need help to make their businesses successful.
That's why my consulting firm was doing very well. People
needed my expertise.

My afternoon client was in a much better position. The
brother was known as "The Kitchen Beautician." He owned a
beauty salon and he was pulling down some serious bank. He

had somewhat of a head for business, because he knew he had the potential to make more money. Women rarely cancelled an appointment with him and he stayed booked up as far out as four weeks. He had a gimmick that made his place the hot spot to be. His beauty salon was too live. It was more than just a place to get your hair done. Women went there to hang out, get advice, gossip, have their wigs washed and they even discussed the latest books and authors on the rise.

"The Kitchen Beautician" made homemade pastries fresh every day for his customers in his kitchen. He was a talented beautician who did women's hair in his kitchen and served them up fresh pastries many wished they could bake themselves. The ladies were instantly attracted to him. He was nice looking and most women found him attractive but quickly knew they didn't have a chance with him as soon as he opened his mouth.

The brother was gay and the sweet tone in his voice raised the gay flag right away. He was open about it and the women were in love with him anyway because he could perform miracles with any length of hair, human or synthetic. That brother could lay a sistah's hair out. I respect him for being open about his sexuality and not trying to be on the "down low" lying to sistahs and endangering their lives.

His business definitely could have been making more money. But he wasn't marketing his business, not even with business cards. He was even doing his own taxes for the business with no tax experience. He had no control over his inventory of hair products and he wanted to open up a second shop. My plan was to help him take his business to the next level by developing an effective marketing strategy. We would start with his already perfect tagline "The Kitchen Beautician" which fit him well.

My business day had gone by faster than I expected it to. I needed to tie up a few last minute things before my workday came to a close. It had been a good day financially on the legit side of the house. However, it had been an extremely lucrative day on the illegal side of the house. Money, who was the guy that watched over my street hustle, called me on my way out of the office. He wanted to let me know that we had pulled down more cash that Monday than we had since we started up, even sweeter than that, it was all tax-free. We only talked briefly. I never talked to him more than a couple of minutes on the phone.

I had just hit the end button on my cell when it started to ring in my hand. It was an unknown number. I assumed it to be the chauffer. I took a deep breath and answered the phone.

"Mr. Johnson speaking," I said. A direct and very professional sounding man was on the other end of the phone.

"Mr. Johnson, this is Evan calling. The chauffer for the limousine you hired. I wanted to let you know that the young lady read the note and declined the limousine Sir. She did write something on the back of the note you had me give to her. Would you like for me to read it?" I told him to read the card but I held my breath.

Mr. Barnes,

I don't want to have any regrets either and for that reason, I can't accept your invitation to dinner. The man I love has my heart and I want him to be able to trust that. You'll understand when you meet the person you want to trust your heart to. Please don't contact me again.
Somara

Listening to him tell me my fate in the note he read is still so clear in my mind. Somara was indeed the woman I had hoped she would be. I could trust her and I decided then that she would be able to trust me as well. I have to admit that I was definitely able to focus better on building both sides of my business.

Things were going extremely well. My girl was loyal and my brother had landed the job he had worked so hard for. My brother was a high-powered defense attorney. My mother had to be happy about that, although, she wouldn't have been happy about some of the things that I was doing. At least, I had kept my promise to her. I had been and would continue to be my brother's keeper.

Chapter 6

Somara and I had been together for over a year. She was in her early thirties and she wanted to have a child. The marriage conversation had come up a few times but I hadn't proposed yet. She said she loved me and she wanted us to have a family together and her desire to have a baby wasn't her way of getting me to propose. I believed her. Somara was not a conniving woman. She had earned my trust several times over.

When we started to discuss having a family, I was proud to be able to say to her that I didn't have any kids out there by anyone. I had definitely had my share of pretty women in between the sheets. After seeing the struggle my mother went through raising Maurice and me, because my absent by choice father walked out on us, I promised myself if I ever had a child, it would be with a woman I planned on staying with.

The housing project I grew up in was filled with single mothers trying to make it. More than a few of their baby daddy's sold mad drugs or had good jobs making good money. They just chose not to take care of their kids. What a sorry excuse for a man. I felt like I had enough past behind me and enough money in my pocket to be a good father. I decided Somara was the woman I wanted to have kids with.

But having a baby turned out to be more than just making a decision because Somara had a very hard time conceiving a child. We tried for over a year. Every month when she got her cycle, I could see the heart breaking disappointment in her eyes. Each time I took her in my arms, held her tightly and whispered in her ear that I loved and adored her with or without a child and that I would always love her. I could feel the sadness in her embrace as she let her body go and sank into my arms. One particular time in a tender voice she said to me, "I love you too baby and I want to feel your love growing inside my body." I wished so much that I could take that hurt away for her. Only God had that power.

We were still happy with the love that we shared and thankful at least that we had found each other. I wanted to do something for Somara to help her relax and take her mind off not getting pregnant, at least for a little while. I called a travel agent and booked a seven-day trip to Aruba. The travel agent sold me on Aruba quickly. The beautiful island in the southern Caribbean, with white sandy private beaches, had my attention the instant she started talking about it.

The dry, warm, sunny climate with its tropical nights, beach barbeques, and ongoing cocktail parties sounded just like what Somara needed. I could imagine us making love in the two bedroom, two bath villa that I rented for us. The first night of lovemaking would have to take place in the huge marble sunken Jacuzzi in the master bedroom.

I had the travel agent leave our travel dates open. I wanted to surprise Somara with the tickets, but I knew she would need to schedule time off work. She liked to travel and had done quite a bit of it. I hadn't traveled outside of Chicago. My plan was to change that by taking Somara somewhere two or three times a year. My paper was long like that and I wanted to start seeing the world. She was the woman I wanted to see it with. I figured we might as well get started on seeing some of the beauty the world had to offer before we had kids.

I couldn't wait to see the excitement on Somara's face when I told her about the trip to Aruba. I made a quick call and asked her to meet me in Millennium Park. The light chill in the air, along with the dust dark of the evening made the park a romantic spot for Somara and I to talk. We liked taking walks together just before the sunset. We did that a lot when we first met. We would walk holding hands and kissing, watching people watch us. I enjoyed the looks of envy I saw in people's faces. Somara got to the park about five thirty in the evening. She was looking like her usual too fine self. Her voice sounded anxious as she greeted me.

"Hey love! How are you? I rushed out of work to get here on time. The tone in your voice sounded a little serious. What's going on?"

I watched Somara's perfectly shaped full lips move as she was talking to me. I was thinking about kissing her as we lay on the pink sandy beach of Aruba. The soft, yellow, and gold sunset on the ocean would pose as our romantic backdrop. "Baby, what are you thinking about?" I remember her asking me. I told her about the trip to Aruba and I wanted us to go as soon as she was able to get time off work. The icing on the cake was me telling her that I was going to buy a house because I wanted us to live together. Her smile got bigger when I told her we would be picking the house out together and I wanted it to be the type of house we could raise a family in.

I don't even know where the house and the living together all came from. That was not what I planned to say. My heart was in control and the words just followed. I felt like it was the right time and the right step for us. Somara's smile and the tears of joy in her eyes, made me feel good.

Somara said she had never been to Aruba but it was one of her dream vacations. Her voice trembled a little bit as she said to me, "Shopping for a house with you, picking out furniture, building a life together, and loving you for a life time is what I want. I love you baby, more today than yesterday, but not as much as I'll love you tomorrow. I want to be all of your tomorrows."

She made me fall in love with her all over again with those words. When my head hit the pillow that night, her beautiful words lingered in my mind as I drifted off to sleep.

Three weeks passed quickly and Somara and I were leaving the next day for Aruba. I had already briefed Denise on the things I needed her to get to my clients in my absence and the couple of power point presentations I prepared and needed her to edit for me. I had two prospective new clients to meet with when I got back from vacation. My business was continuing to grow. I felt really good about that.

My desire to get out of the dope game was real. I was encouraged by the success of my consulting firm and that it would be my way out. But things kept happening that wouldn't let the hold the dope game had on me go. Money was the only guy in my circle of illegal business associates that I came close to trusting. I said close, I didn't trust him fully either. I felt like my lack of trust was one of the reasons why I had been able to stay under the radar of the police.

Money called me about a week after I booked the trip to Aruba. I wasn't expecting to hear from him for a couple of days when it was time to settle up for the week. But he told me one of his boys had been stuck up for a Kilo of cocaine. That was a lot of money. I considered taking my suit off and stepping hard to somebody. There was no way; I would take that kind of loss or that type of disrespect. But I had played it smart up to that point and I needed to keep my head on straight and my hands as clean as possible. I had Money put the word out on the street that the dope or its value in money needed to be replaced. The loss wouldn't be taken without somebody suffering some consequences.

The night before Somara and I were scheduled to leave for Aruba, Money called me to say he handled things with the cocaine that was stolen. He didn't have the product but he had its value in cash. I met him at our usual spot and he handed the cash off to me. At the time I was impressed with his quick response in dealing with the situation and I felt like he had my back. But I would later learn that the only thing he had for my back was a knife.

I shielded Somara from the ugly side of the handsome man she said she looked at once and knew she wanted to love past anything she ever felt for any other man. At least that's what she told me. Up to that point, I had been able to keep Somara from knowing about the dark side of what I did for a living. I knew that would be more difficult to do once we started living together. I didn't want her or the child we hoped to have to be touched by any of that ugly stuff. My plans for Somara and I to live together gave new energy to my commitment to get on the legal side of the law. I was anxious to take a break from even thinking about it all.

We had an early morning flight that landed in Aruba before nine thirty. The hot 80-degree weather was a welcomed change from the early winter winds that we left behind in Chicago. The crystal clear blue water from the calm ocean that rolled in on the private beach of our villa was a gorgeous sight. It set the tone for what would turn out to be a more than unforgettable vacation.

Our third day on the island started with a soft yellow sunrise, a mild breeze, and the sweet, clean, smell of Somara's hair that fell over her face as she slept. I laid there next to her waiting for her to wake up. Fresh strawberries, peaches and whipped cream, buttery flaky croissants, havarti cheese, thinly sliced smoked ham, eggs, orange juice and coffee waited to be served on the balcony for her as soon as she woke up.

When She opened her eyes, the look on her face was priceless. She was very surprised that I had taken charge and was taking care of her. No matter what time I got up in the morning, I always waited for her to fix us breakfast. She would jokingly tell me that was why she didn't sleep over at my apartment more often.

We had a day filled with adventures. Parasailing, hang gliding and scuba diving had us both drained by the end of the day. We used muscles that we forgot we had. My eyes were the only part of my body that wasn't tired. That was because I was enjoying the sight of Somara wearing the hell out of that two-piece bikini she bought on the island. Her 34-D cup, plump breast had my full attention.

The night was calm and belonged to us alone. The picnic under the stars on the private beach of our villa blew Somara away. She was right; I had never been so romantic. Being with her in such a beautiful place made me feel like Somara and I were in our own little world. I looked forward to our last few days on the island. We would be going home soon. But thoughts of going home and leaving what felt like paradise were bitter sweet.

We spent the next couple of days sight seeing, shopping, eating way too much food and trying to burn it off by making love on the beach at night. Underneath the stars, life seemed endless. Touching her, kissing her, and feeling her warm body underneath mine, as she moved gently, drove me crazy. It was our last night on the island and we made love over and over again.

We boarded our return flight home and were quickly seated in first class. Somara and I drank champagne. I was already thinking about where I could take her on our next trip. Somara's bright eyes, glowing skin, and the beautiful smile on her face told me she was rested and happy. That had been my goal for her and I wanted to out do myself with the next trip. I didn't know where that would be. But I knew I would be using the same travel agent. She had definitely made sure that my money had been well spent on our Aruba paradise.

I was thankful for the smooth flight home, since it was five hours long. It was Sunday night and Somara didn't have to be back at work until Tuesday. I was going into the office on Monday. Somara would be at my apartment when I got back from the office. She planned on looking through the real estate section of the Sunday paper and a few interior design magazines. She was excited about house shopping. She made me promise to help her pick out the furniture. She didn't have to work too hard at it. My promise to her came willingly.

Chapter 7

A couple of months had passed since our trip to Aruba. The harsh winter winds of the windy city were living up to their reputation. Chicago is a beautiful city, even more so at Christmas. Downtown Chicago becomes a magical Christmas menagerie. The lights, decorations, Macy's window dressings, and of course the huge Christmas tree at Daley Center is what makes Christmas beautiful in the city. The famous annual Christmas tree lighting ceremony in early December is the official kick off of the holiday season in Chicago.

Somara and I had happily shivered in the cold drinking hot chocolate, as we watched the Christmas tree lighting and the fireworks that followed. I took her to dinner at the Cheesecake Factory. After dinner we went back to my apartment. Almost immediately Somara was in the shower. I figured she was tired and wanted to get to bed early. To my unexpected pleasure, when I got out of the shower, she was lying in front of the fireplace in a gorgeous, sexy, long white silk gown that I hadn't seen before. The lace that bordered the plunging V neckline seductively caressed her full firm breast, which was exactly what I planned on doing.

Vanilla scented candles lit the room. The musical serenade of Anita Baker and Gerald Levert made me think of the first time I met her. She was beautiful then and even more beautiful as I looked at her lying in front of the fireplace, making me appreciate her soft smile, warm loving gaze, and luscious curves and hips. Plump, sweet strawberries with whipped cream and champagne sat on a sliver tray next to her.

She handed me a pretty red box with a white bow. There was something different about her smile and the way she looked at me. There was such a peaceful expression on her face. But there was even something about her all together that just seemed different. I untied the bow, lifted the top off of the box, and immediately my heart began to race. I swallowed hard as I looked up into Somara's eyes. She leaned close to me and whispered in my ear, "I don't know if it's a girl or a boy, but we're having a baby." The box held two baby rattles, one pink and one blue.

I was ecstatic! My baby was having my baby. The look in her eyes that I couldn't explain was something more than happiness. It was joy! She was glowing. Somara was about eight weeks pregnant. Our baby had been conceived in Aruba. I didn't need anything else for Christmas. She had just given me all that I needed and wanted. I kissed Somara passionately and told her how much I loved her and how much her being pregnant meant to me. Her soft sweet words sent my mind spinning into the future.

Tears were already rolling down her face when she said, "I love you and I knew when I first met you, you were the man that I wanted to spend the rest of my life with. Now our love has created another life. Don't ever leave me baby."

"I promise, I'll never leave you." Those words were easy for me to say. That was how I felt about her. She was definitely my future. I couldn't help myself. I had to start right away buying just a few things that I wanted my son to have before he was even born. I wanted a boy but a beautiful healthy little girl that looked like Somara was more than fine with me.

Chicago Bulls and Bears season tickets were a few years too early to buy. But that was definitely my plan for my son and I. Savings bonds and a little pair of Nike gym shoes had to be under the Christmas for my baby. I also wanted to have a huge present under the tree for Somara. Unfortunately, a house would be a little bit of a tight fit.

Somara and I had been looking at houses for about three weeks. We saw two that she fell in love with right away. She was concerned that we might not be able to comfortably afford the mortgage. I knew that would not be a problem. I also knew that I couldn't tell her just how long my money was, not without having to explain how I had become so financially secure. I was however contemplating what I could tell her that would be believable when it came to buying her the house she wanted.

It was a week before Christmas and we looked at five houses that week. Two of them, we had looked at previously. They were the two houses that Somara had fallen in love with. I was trying to get her to tell me on the sly which one she liked the best. I wanted her to see them again because one of them would be her Christmas gift. That's why I needed her to walk through every room of each house one last time.

Christmas Eve came quickly and I had already given Denise the gifts I bought her boys Kyle and Kevin. I didn't tell Denise that the two large beautifully wrapped boxes I had delivered to her house held a 54-inch flat screen TV and a Nintendo Wii game for her boys.

They didn't ask me for either gift. When I asked them what they wanted for Christmas, their response was clothes. Kevin and Kyle were good boys and I was sure they would have thought it was too much for them to ask me for. But I heard them talking to their mom about a Wii game and trying to make a deal with her about keeping their rooms clean, not bickering with each other and getting only A's and B's in school. I figured they would enjoy the game better with a bigger TV.

Denise asked me what I was giving Somara for Christmas and that gave me a chance to ask her what she was getting her sons. So, I knew the Nintendo Wii game was not on the list of things she planned to get them. Denise's two round trip tickets to Belize and a weeks stay at a five star hotel would keep her from feeling left out on Christmas.

The card with her gift said *Merry Christmas Mom. We love you!* I didn't get a chance to do something like that for my mom. But I could look out for Denise and that made me feel good. It was things like that, which helped me justify why being in the dope game wasn't wrong.

Maurice was out of college and had landed a great job. Even though he didn't need my money anymore, I had become accustom to a certain life style and the financial freedom that allowed me to be able to say, "I'll take that Mercedes, that house and by the way, I want the keys to the house to be plated in real gold." I didn't have to ask how much it would cost. I just had to say when I wanted to take possession.

That's exactly what I did. I told the realtor I wanted the closing paperwork on the house done and in Somara's name by December 24th. I wanted to be able to take her to our new home on Christmas morning. I bought one and only one piece of furniture for the house. A king size mahogany wood bed with a pillow top mattress that sat on the podium in the master bedroom. The four steps it took to walk up to the top of the podium definitely made the bed a centerpiece in the room.

I wanted to be able to make love to Somara in front of the fireplace. The only thing I wanted in the bedroom was the bed, the fireplace blazing, and a silver-serving tray with champagne and chocolate dipped strawberries. The bedroom already had a wall-to-wall built in sound system. Everything else I wanted Somara and I to pick out together. I knew she would want to finish off our bedroom and then furnish the nursery before we even bought furniture for the rest of the house. I didn't care. Whatever she wanted to do was fine with me.

Maurice was in town from Atlanta for Christmas. Somara bought him a monogrammed leather brief case and 14K gold Parker Chiseled black fountain pen. She had his name engraved on the pen in real gold lettering. Somara was definitely a classy woman and she knew how to give classy gifts. She spent a week shopping for him. I was looking forward to seeing the look on Maurice's face when he opened his gifts.

Of course, I had to get him a really nice gift too. Although Maurice lived in Atlanta, he was still a Bulls and Bears fan. That meant season tickets to both would be a gift he and I could enjoy together.

I was anxious about Christmas morning just like a kid. I don't know why I had such a crazy dream on Christmas Eve. It was late when I went to bed. Somara was already sleeping. She was just past the first trimester and she was starting to get a little baby bump in her stomach and she needed her rest. I laid down next to her until she fell asleep. Then I got up, read a little, and went over the books for my consulting firm. I had a good accountant, but you better believe, I still watched my money closely. I could never understand why a person would just trust someone else to tell them how much money they had.

My money was piling up. I needed to start thinking about investing in real estate; money markets or stocks, something that would make my money keep growing legally. The time would come for me to get out of the game. I wanted to get out and be financially set for life and that would require my being smart; smart enough to do something with my money that would keep making money and not get me taken down before I decided to get out of the game.

After the holidays, I planned on buying up a few more rental properties. I knew it would be unbelievable to the Fed's that I owned nothing in my name. I felt I needed to purchase a couple of small rental properties in my name alone. They would generate monthly revenue and help to legitimize my income.

The purchases would also continue to lend to an increased cash flow that would look good on paper to Somara. I didn't want her sweat'n me about how we were able to live the way we did. I also planned on putting some of that property solely in her name. Since we weren't married yet, if the Feds took me down, they couldn't take everything I had.

When I finally went to bed, sleep came over me easily. I dreamed Somara was about seven months pregnant. I can even remember how soft the brown skin on her plump belly was in my dream. She was full of my baby. In the dream, I was snuggled up close behind her with my arms wrapped around her stomach. I could feel our baby moving in her belly. I remember thinking to myself that my son would be set for life the day he was born. He wouldn't have to take any risk to secure his future. I had taken enough risk for all of us.

I go to sleep sometimes now in my cell embracing that dream in my mind, hoping that when I fall asleep, I can dream the same dream again. But I would want the ending to be different.

In my dream, I was just about to fall asleep when I inhaled Somara's perfume and kissed the back of her neck. It was at that second that my life took an explosive turn. The Fed's kicked in my front door and swarmed my house like unwanted roaches when you turn on the lights. I was dragged from the bed with Somara and thrown to the floor by two men who handcuffed me so tight my wrist bled. Another man pulled Somara from the bed and stood her against the wall.

A sharp pain pierced my chest as I yelled as loudly and forcefully as I could for no one to touch her. I could feel myself saying, "You can see she's pregnant and nothing better happen to her or my child." The blow to my head with what I think was a heavy metal flashlight knocked me out. As

I fell to the floor, I could feel the warm red blood that trickled down the side of my face. When my body hit the floor, in the dream, I woke up.

The dream had seemed so shockingly real. I looked over to make sure Somara was lying in bed next to me. I touched her, kissed her and caressed her pregnant belly. That was the only way I could tell the difference between the dream and reality. The paralyzing pain that had just shot through my head seemed like it had all really happened.

I took a deep breath and inhaled the sweet smell of Somara's perfume. I ran my hand down her arm caressing her soft skin. I held her tightly as the reality of my dream reminded me that my dream could very well come true if I wasn't careful and wise enough to get out of the game. That dream was like my wake up call. I knew I needed to expedite my exit plan.

Chapter 8

Snow covered the tree branches, housetops, and the ground. It was still pure white and undisturbed. Big snowflakes were falling that set the perfect background for Christmas morning. It was early and the dark haze of night hadn't been parted by the sunrise yet. Looking out of the window at the snow-covered world was like looking at a picture. The only thing missing was a snowman sitting in the yard, wearing a black top hat, a carrot for his nose, buttons for his eyes, and a red wool scarf wrapped around his neck. I planned to make sure that snowman had a chance to come to life in my front yard. Me, Somara and our child would build him together.

The voices blasting through the surround sound system of my TV interrupted my daydreams of a Christmas that was yet to come. The TV was set to come on every morning with the six o'clock channel 5 news. The weather forecast was for a chilly 22 degrees with another two feet of snow to fall. That would make the white blanket of snow that covered the ground a total of three and a half feet for Christmas day. I watched the news for about thirty minutes before I fell back to sleep. I hoped that there wouldn't be too much ugly news to report on such a clean white day in the city. But unfortunately the ugly things in life don't stop. Not even for a beautiful snowy white Christmas day.

When I woke up again it was after nine o'clock. Somara moved away from my tight embrace to answer the phone. It was Maurice calling to tell us, "Merry Christmas." He had just landed at the airport and was on his way over to my apartment. He, Somara and I were going to have breakfast. We got up, showered, and dressed. Somara wanted me to open one of my gifts before Maurice got there. She handed me a box wrapped in dark blue and white gift-wrapping paper with a big with bow. I was sure that the blue gift-wrapping paper was not by chance. Especially since Somara knew blue to be my favorite color.

The box held a high definition digital camcorder for recording our family memories. She told me I could record our baby's birth. But she made me swear that only she and I could look at it. I had mentioned to her a couple of weeks before Christmas that I was going to buy one because; I didn't want to miss any of our baby's precious moments. So her gift was perfect. I remember pulling her close to me as I whispered in her ear that she was just what I needed in my life.

A knock on the door with a familiar rhythmic tap told me it was Maurice. That had been our little secret knock since we were kids. Maurice walked through the door loaded down with a matching leather garment and duffle bag and a huge fruit basket. He knew Somara loved fruit.

A couple of hours went by quickly. Breakfast, conversation and the gift exchange eased us into early afternoon. I told Maurice I wanted to take him to see the house I bought for Somara and me before he left town and about my plan to give her a private viewing of the house later that day. We spent some more time talking about the baby and the fact that Maurice was finally going to be an uncle. He seemed pretty excited about that.

Denise and her boys called to say, "Merry Christmas" and to thank me for the Christmas gifts. I could hardly understand the first minute of the conversation with her boys. Kyle and Kevin were both talking at the same time and the excitement in their voices was unmistakable. They wanted me to come over and play the Nintendo Wii game with them. Denise was in tears as she thanked me for her gift. She said she had never traveled out of Chicago. She talked to Somara for a few minutes also to thank her. My girl Somara was unbelievably secure. Any other woman would have had a fit if her man gave another woman an all expenses paid vacation.

Maurice wanted to spend some time visiting a few of his boys that still lived in the city. He would be back to have dinner with Somara and me. She had cooked enough food for a small army. I asked her why did she cook such a large buffet of food. She laughed and said, "It's the holidays and you always have to be prepared for unexpected visitors." Anybody who stopped by unexpectedly could eat all they wanted, except there wouldn't be any sweet potato pie to be dished up for anyone. I had eaten half a pie already and the other two were going to be stashed away in my private little hiding place.

Christmas day was passing and I had given Somara a couple of nice gifts, but not the gold plated house key. I told Somara that I left her big gift at my office and I wanted her to ride along with me to pick it up. When she realized we weren't going to my office, I handed her the box that held the gold house key and told her not to open it. We drove for another twenty-five minutes before I parked about a block down the street from the house I purchased for us.

I told Somara she could open the box. With a puzzled looked on her face she picked up the dangling gold key. Smiling, she asked me why did I give her a key? I took the key from Somara and told her the box was supposed to hold a three-carat diamond tennis bracelet. The jeweler made a mistake and gave me someone else's box.

Her smile and the gleam in her eyes faded a little with the discovery of the mistake she thought the jeweler had made. I kissed her and told her we would go to the jewelers on Monday and get her bracelet. I promised that she would end up with a bigger surprise than she expected.

I asked Somara if it would be okay if I picked up something from a client, whose house we were parked just down the street from. She protested slightly because it was Christmas, and then reluctantly agreed. I opened her car door and held her close to me as we walked up the sidewalk.

When we got to the house, Somara noticed the sold sign in the yard. The disappointment was obvious in her voice as she said, "Someone bought our house. I wanted us to have that house." I kissed her and promised that she would be happy with the house we would end up with. I rang the doorbell twice. Somara suggested that we leave since there was probably no one home. I asked her for the key she had gotten by mistake then I pulled her into my arms, holding her tightly, I kissed her. My tongue gently parted her lips and the taste of her sweet, moist tongue satisfied my craving to kiss her. I unlocked the door with the key and pushed it open. I lifted Somara up in my arms and carried her through the doorway.

The look in her eyes when I said, "Welcome home love" was priceless. She started to cry, which I knew she would do. I felt like our future together had a formal start at that very moment. We walked through the house together and talked about how to decorate each room. I made sure the master bedroom was the last stop.

Maurice was happy to stop by the house before we got there. I had him leave a heart shaped box of chocolate dipped strawberries and an ice bucket with two bottles of non-alcoholic sparkling cider. It also gave him a chance to have a sneak preview of the house. He cared a lot for Somara and he was happy to see me letting my heart go with her.

It was almost seven o'clock in the evening when we got back to my apartment. We had intended to make love in every room of the new house. But the bed and fireplace in the master bedroom just wouldn't let us go. We would have to take care of the other rooms once we moved into the house.

Christmas evening was filled with whispers of years past and the hopes and dreams of many happy years yet to come that Somara and I would spend together with our children. We both fell asleep talking about what we would name our baby.

The day after Christmas didn't start with just lightly falling snow. It also started with me waking up in bed alone. Somara had gotten out of bed but left behind a letter on her pillow. For a second, I was motionless with apprehension about what could be in the letter. But I quickly dismissed my concern. The letter smelled of Somara's favorite perfume, Issey Miyake. The cherry red lipstick kiss on the envelope made me long for Somara's sweet delicious lips. As I read the letter, I felt her love for me in every word.

Sweetheart,

You are indeed my heart's desire! To say that I love you seems so inadequate some how. Only you could make the cherished and sought after words "I love you" seem insufficient. But I do love you. I love you beyond my heart and to the very essence of who I am. Please believe that your love alone was Christmas gift enough for me. I was prepared to continue house hunting with you. I didn't think that we could afford the house that I really wanted. That was why I didn't say too much when the realtor told us the selling price.

So the shock of you buying such a gorgeous house, the one I wanted, giving me a gold plated key, and having it all done to surprise me for Christmas was unbelievable.

Some people believe in luck or fate. I believe that what God has for you is for you. It is not by chance, luck, or fate that we are together. I cannot imagine loving any man in this lifetime but you. There have been many times in my life that I have felt lonely and wished that I hadn't been an only child. It took me so many years to learn to live with my parents being killed in a car accident when I was six. I never felt like a whole person after that.

Of course, something in my life was always missing. You and only you have come close to making me feel whole again. You have made this a Christmas that I will forever hold dear. Thank you for being the man that you are. My heart is now and forever yours. My precious love know that I love you more today than yesterday but not as much as I will love you tomorrow.

Kisses!

Somara

Chapter 9

January was almost over and the holiday for lovers was right around the corner. I was still trying to figure out what I wanted to do for Somara for Valentine's Day. She was five and half months pregnant and still gorgeous. Somara worked out and paid close attention to what she ate. Except for the bulge in her stomach, you could hardly tell she was pregnant. She said she had too many clothes she would have to replace if she didn't get back down to her pre-baby weight. She was very determined to be healthy and not gain any unnecessary weight.

I hadn't been sleeping a lot and I was preoccupied with keeping things under control. I had some trouble with a couple of my spots being robbed and the cops kicking in the door. I felt that I had built enough layers between myself, and the front line of my dope business, that if anything happened it couldn't touch me. The business would go down, but I would still be left standing. But the reality of what was going on in the streets definitely had my attention. Between that and Somara not feeling well I was pretty preoccupied. At least we had already moved into our house and were close to being finished with the furniture buying and decorating.

For about a week, Somara had been feeling some pressure and cramps in her stomach. I went to the doctor with her. She had an ultra sound that didn't uncover the reason for her pain and discomfort. She was still working, but I was taking her to work and picking her up that particular week. Her doctor didn't want her driving and nor did I.

It was Thursday and I was glad Somara's work week was almost over. I wanted her to spend the rest of the week at home relaxing. I tried to get her to take Friday off and we could have a long weekend at home enjoying each other. She said she had a project at work that needed her attention. However, she promised she would take a couple of days off the following week.

I was sitting in the parking lot waiting for Somara to get off work. My boy Anthony called me and I was on the phone with him about fifteen minutes. I looked at the clock on my dashboard and realized Somara had already been off work for ten minutes. In my rear view mirror, I noticed her about to walk down the steps of her building. I hurried to get out of the car and get to her. I had intended to be standing at the door to help her down the steps. I was half way across the parking lot when I noticed a guy who looked like he was pacing his brisk walk in order to meet Somara when she got to the bottom of the steps.

He started to run toward her. I called out to Somara. As she looked in my direction, I saw the man push her down and grab her purse all in one motion.

My heart was pounding so hard, I could hear it in my ears and my chest felt like it was about to explode. I watched her body fall to the ground. She fell on her stomach and in her scream I heard the pain she must have felt. I was running fast and I had almost reached her when she called out my name and my heart broke. I knew at that instant she was going to lose our baby. When I got to Somara, I could see the blood already soaking through her light tan maternity dress. She cried out in pain and clinched my arm as I sat there on the sidewalk holding her body next to mine. I called 911 on my cell phone.

Two women walking out of the building ran down the steps to help us. I put my coat over Somara and one of the ladies gave me a coat to put underneath her head. I didn't want to release her from my arms. The first woman who rushed to help us said it might ease the pain for Somara to lie down flat.

The other lady put her coat on top of mine and started to rub Somara's legs.

I heard the siren from the ambulance screeching. It was only then that I looked over at the crowd of people down toward the end of the sidewalk, and realized that someone had tackled the man who knocked Somara to the ground. There were several people holding him down and yelling out, "Don't worry man, we got him." I didn't care about that man at all. He had already done irreparable damage.

As the ambulance raced through red lights, I felt like my pulse raced at the same speed. I knew in my heart that the baby wasn't going to make it. It wasn't long after we got to the hospital that my fear became a reality. The doctor told me he couldn't save the baby but Somara would be fine, I was speechless for a minute. I opened my mouth to ask if Somara would be able to have more children. Before I could get the words out, the doctor put his firm hand on my shoulder and said, "You'll be able to try again. Just give her a little time."

I stood at the window in the waiting room looking out at the black night. I needed to collect myself before I could see Somara. I searched my heart and my mind for the words to say to her. I walked into the recovery room. She was still sleeping. I sat in the chair next to her bed. I held her hand and

I very much wanted her to wake up and know that I was there with her. I so dreaded the pain that I knew I would see in her eyes.

After an hour of sitting next to Somara's bed and fighting to hold back my own tears, she finally woke up. She looked at me as she took both her hands and touched her stomach. Tears washed down her face and her broken heart poured out right along with them. All I could do was hold her in my arms and tell her how much I loved her. Her voice was shaky and soft when she said to me, "I know in my heart that we will never have another a child." I tried to reassure her that we would and that everything would work out. She continued to cry and my heart broke with every tear that fell. Somara was inconsolable.

She was in the hospital four days. I took everything out of the baby's room before I picked her up from the hospital. I didn't want her to have to come home and put all of her dreams of having a baby into a box.

A couple of months passed and Somara still didn't have the sparkle in her eyes that I was used to seeing, but I could hear in her voice that it was possible. We had started to talk a little about when we might try again to have a child. Those conversations gave us both hope. As we worked our way through the healing process our love for each other was strengthened. While I tried to be strong for her, she was trying to be strong for me. My love for Somara continued to grow. When I thought there was no way for me to love her more, She would always do or say something that just made my heart melt.

A week later another tragedy would grip my heart. At one o'clock in the morning a ringing phone told me before I even answered it that I was about to be told something horrible. The voice on the other end of the phone verified my fears. "I'm Dr. Holmgren with Emory University Hospital in Atlanta Georgia. Are you Malcolm and do you know a Maurice Johnson? Your name was the first name in his cell phone. He's in critical condition in ICU." Those words were like physical blows to my body. I felt sick to my stomach.

I woke Somara and told her that Maurice had been in a serious car accident and he was in ICU. I hated to leave Somara since she was still so fragile and she needed me. But she didn't surprise me when she got up and started calling the airlines to book me on the first possible flight to Atlanta. She said she would go to work and tie up a few things and she would be on a plane the next day to Atlanta. Her actions were just another one of those things she did that made me love her so much.

I packed a bag and got on the 5:30 a.m. flight to Atlanta. I watched the clouds move by my window seat. I thought for sure in the clouds I could see images of Maurice and me when we were kids. I could see Maurice standing on the porch looking like his best friend had left him behind every time I ran off to play with my friends and didn't let him tag along. I could even see the smile of victory on his face when I cornered the bully down the street that kept picking on him. I closed my eyes and the images of our childhood faded. But the fear in my heart and mind that I might lose my brother was clearly before me.

The flight lasted a little over two hours. I hurried through the airport to locate ground travel. Then I grabbed a taxi and went straight to the hospital. I made a quick call to Somara before I reached the hospital to make sure she was okay and let her know I had landed safely. With every step toward the hospital entrance I prayed God would not take my brother's life. I felt a little uncomfortable praying because it was not something that I did a lot of. I knew I shouldn't only pray when I needed something from God and for that reason I hoped God would hear my prayer.

I stopped at the information desk to find out where ICU was located. While I rode the elevator up to the fourth floor, I was still praying. Locating the nurses' station, getting an update on Maurice, and finding out when I could go in to see him, all happened without me even realizing my actions. I knew what I had to do and it was like it was all happening without my body moving or my mind processing any thoughts.

The moment I stepped into that cold ICU and saw all the monitors and wires hooked up to Maurice, I thought of my mother. The chill in the air the night she died. The cold pavement that couldn't soak up the warm blood that oozed from her body. I couldn't hold back the tears. Seeing Maurice lying there took me back to when my mom died and my brother needed me. I was all he had then and I was there for him. I knew I had to be there for him again.

I spent the next thirty minutes talking to Maurice and holding his hand. I didn't know if he could hear me or not. I think I needed to hear the words I said to him as much as I thought he needed to hear them. I told Maurice that I loved him and I would do what ever it took, no matter how much it cost to make sure he was okay. Reminding him about the season tickets to the Chicago Bulls and Bears games that we still had to take advantage of, gave me something to look forward to with him. I hoped he could hear me. I didn't want those season tickets to be the last Christmas gift that I ever gave him.

Maurice's doctor came in to give me the details about his condition. Looking into his fixed stern expression told me that the situation was grave. Maurice had a collapsed lung, the femur bone in his thigh was broken and his back. He was in a comma due to the swelling of his brain. The doctor wasn't sure if there would be any brain damage or not. We had to wait until the swelling went down for the doctor to make that determination. The doctor said a man driving a BMW, ran a red light going sixty-five miles an hour, while he was arguing with his girlfriend. They were both killed. Maurice had been driving an SUV, I didn't know if that was why he had survived or not. I was however grateful that my brother was still with me.

I made some calls back to Chicago. I needed to make sure that my business was covered. I would be out of town until I knew where things stood with Maurice. I planned on taking him back to Chicago with me to recover. I also called Somara and told her not to come down to Atlanta. I wanted her at home safe and resting. I told her my plan to bring Maurice back with me when he was able to travel. I would be back to fly her down with me as soon as I could. I didn't want her traveling by herself and I didn't want her alone for too long. She wanted to be with me but she said she understood.

Maurice had been in the hospital for about a week when I flew back to Chicago. I picked up Somara and we flew down to Atlanta together. She talked to the doctors and found out what type of after care Maurice would need.

She called her friend who was the Chief of Staff at one of the leading research hospitals in Los Angeles for a second opinion. He spent an hour on a conference call with Somara and me making sure that we understood everything that Maurice's doctor told us. He agreed with the doctor's recommendations and referred us to a facility for physical therapy in Chicago. He said they were the best but they were expensive. I told him cost would not be the barrier between Maurice and a hundred percent recovery.

Two weeks had passed and Somara and I were still in Atlanta. Maurice's apartment was spotless, the newspaper had been cancelled and the refrigerator cleaned out. Somara even got his mail forwarded to our address in Chicago. She thought about things I would have walked away and left undone. I was so glad she was there with me. I needed her and I knew it. You can believe I had no problem telling her that. After being in Atlanta over a week with me, she had to get back to Chicago for work. Time seemed to pass much slower after she left.

Almost a month after Maurice's accident he and I were on board a private medical flight to Chicago. An ambulance met us at O'Hare airport and we headed to my house with him. Somara helped me take care of my brother like he was her own. Taking care of him was almost therapeutic for her and it gave them a chance to get to know each a lot better.

Several weeks passed and Maurice was feeling much better but he still had limited physical capabilities. His doctor had given us a hopeful prognosis for a full recovery. It would just take some time, a lot of hard work on Maurice's part, and quite a bit of money. His medical insurance paid for some of the expenses. But not the quality of care I wanted him to have. I was determined that he would have the best care money could buy. I was willing to spend every dime I had to make that happen.

Three months went by with Maurice continuing to get stronger and gain more and more strength in his back and legs. The stronger he got, the more focused he was on getting back to work. His law firm assured him that he had nothing to worry about. One of the partners called at least once every two weeks to see how he was doing. He said Maurice was a valued attorney and they needed him back in the office, as soon as he was ready. That news kept Maurice's spirits up.

I was glad that he had something to hold on to, something that would keep the fight in him. Since Maurice was doing much better, Somara and I started talking about the finishing touches we still needed to do around the house. She sounded excited when we talked about the framed art, furniture for my office, and the guest bedroom that still had to be picked out. She hadn't been excited about much since we lost the baby. It was good to see some happiness in her face again.

Chapter 10

Maurice was healthy and had been back at work for a few months. That would soon benefit me in a not so unexpected way. A dream I had became an ugly reality that opened the door to the cellblock that I would soon reside on. When the Fed's first kicked in my front door, and swarmed my house like unwanted roaches do when you turn on the lights, it made me think back to a dream in which the exact same thing happened. The real events were so close to what happened in my dream; I couldn't believe the insanity of it all was really happening.

I was dragged from the bed with Somara and thrown to the floor by two men who handcuffed me so tightly my wrist bled. Another man pulled Somara from the bed and stood her against the wall. A sharp pain pierced my chest as I yelled as loudly and forcefully as I could, "No one better touch her. You can see she's pregnant and nothing better happen to her or my child." I could feel my lips moving and I could hear the sound of my voice. Suddenly, I realized that in the dream she was pregnant. But this was reality. Somara wasn't pregnant and I was really going to jail.

I felt my heart pounding in my chest. The blow to my head with what I think was a heavy metal flashlight knocked me out. As I fell to the floor, I could feel the warm red blood that trickled down the side of my face. When my body hit the floor in the dream, I woke up. But when my body hit the floor this time, it wasn't a dream and when I woke up I was in the jail infirmary.

It took me a couple of minutes to realize where I was. Then the reality of what happened sobered my thoughts quickly. I called out for someone and a tall slim nurse came in. I asked where was Somara and was she okay. The woman said she didn't know what I was talking about, but she would get a guard for me. A big huskie man with a gun strapped on his side and a look on his face that told me he didn't appreciate being annoyed said,

"I don't want any trouble out of you. You'll be arraigned in the morning."

"I need to make a phone call," I told him.

"When you're released from the infirmary, you can make your phone call," was the stern response he gave me.

Looking into his ice-cold eyes, I knew no level of verbal persistence would get me the phone call I wanted. Before the next morning came, the minutes passed like hours and the hours passed like days. I didn't sleep much. I saw Somara's face whether my eyes were open or closed. I needed to know she was okay. I also knew she needed me to explain to her why and what had just happened to us. A secret that I had so successfully hidden from her, an ugly secret that had brought both of us to a crossroads in our lives had been uncovered.

I tried to find the words that I would need to explain the mess that I had gotten us both into. But no combination of words seemed to make sense. What could I have said to Somara that would have explained why I jeopardized our home, our future and even our lives? I could have told her the night my mother was killed, I promised myself I would take care of Maurice. I could have told her how difficult it was financially. I could have even told her that I had decided to get out of the game within a few months but when Maurice almost died in that car accident his medical care strained my funds significantly. I just needed a little time to stack my money again. Then I would have gotten out.

I also wanted her to know that it was my desire that she not have to work. I wanted her to be able to stay at home and just take care of all the kids we wanted to have. I wasn't sure that any of that would keep me from losing Somara.

It was finally morning and two guards came to the infirmary. I asked for my phone call. One of the guards told me I could make my call right after I talked with my attorney who was waiting to see me. I didn't ask any questions. I didn't know who the attorney was and it didn't matter. I needed one and I was glad to even hear the word attorney. The guard led me into a private holding room and pushed me down into a chair. My hands were still handcuffed behind me. He told me my attorney would be right in. Then he took the handcuffs off me. I remember rubbing my wrist and feeling the deep marks, almost cuts the handcuffs had made on them.

Ten long minutes later, a well dressed, nice looking man was escorted through the door. The guard told him to just call out when he was ready to leave. His eyes looked forgiving and his embrace gave me strength. I opened my mouth and almost got out the words "I'm sorry," when Maurice put his hand on my shoulder and said, "Man, I don't care what you did. I love you and I got your back! That's all that matters." I looked at my little brother. I think for the first time, I didn't see my little brother, I saw a man. He hugged me again and assured me that things would work out. Maurice quickly got down to business. We had a lot to talk about.

Maurice told me Somara called to tell him that I had been arrested and he took the next flight out to Chicago. I asked him how she was and if she was furious with me. He assured me she was okay. I was relieved to hear him say, "She's not furious. Somara's worried about you and what she should expect. She doesn't care what you did or why you did it. She just wants you home with her."

I told Maurice, I was trying to figure out a way to explain to Somara why I had chosen such a destructive pathway. No words seemed adequate and I felt that she wouldn't understand.

Maurice put his hand on my shoulder, which felt as comforting as the words that came out of his mouth. "I already told her that I was pretty sure your unyielding drive for me to have everything I needed, for us to get out of the projects, and for me to have a degree in my hand was the start of it all." That was true but I didn't want my brother to dislike the man I had become.

I started to try to explain to him how it all started. He interrupted me to let me know he already understood. "You were a young kid, not much older than me, but you made it for both of us. I didn't know that you were into dealing drugs. Maybe I just didn't want to know. But when Somara called me, I put it all together. Just like you did what ever you needed to do for me then, I'm here now, and I'm going to do what ever I have to do for you to make this okay."

Fighting back the tears in my eyes, I told my brother how much I loved him. He said, "I love you big brother. I got you." I asked him how long could he stay in town. He told me he would be with me until it was over. He was going to stay at the house with Somara. I was really glad to hear that. Maurice spent the next hour asking me questions, telling me what to expect, and talking about how he planned on putting my defense together.

Maurice set up a visit for Somara and me. I expected to see disappointment in her eyes. What I saw was only love and concern. She wasn't angry with me for doing something so foolish; she didn't hate me for jeopardizing what we had and even who we were together. She never even asked me if I did it or not. She just wanted us to go home together. I guess in the scheme of things I shouldn't have been surprised at her response to it all. She had been in my corner always, from day one.

Somara did, however, surprise me with what she told me about Maurice. When he asked his firm for time off because his brother needed an attorney, the firm questioned him about what type of case it was he would be taking on. Maurice's firm represented mostly white-collar crime, embezzlement, fraud that type of stuff. When Maurice was honest about my case being a drug case, the partners told him his involvement would have a negative effect on the firm. They gave him a choice, represent me or keep his job. Maurice cleaned out his office and got on a plane to Chicago.

The next few months were beyond hard. Maurice and I worked on building my defense while I tried to figure out who it was in my camp that had designed the downfall of my empire. But I had to get out of jail first. I had a million dollar bond which meant it would cost me a $100,000 to walk. None of that money could come from any of my assets or even the legitimate bank account that was associated with my consulting firm. The Fed's had seized my assets and my bank accounts. Somara used some of the money from the trust fund her parents left her for my bond. Two days after being arrested my bail was posted.

The thought of putting my hands on the man that had betrayed me was as important to me as beating the drug case I was faced with. I felt pretty confident that somebody who knew me had to help the Fed's bring me down. Once I was home with Somara my heart changed. Looking into her eyes and holding her warm body next to mine every night made me realize that I had already done enough to jeopardize our life together. Without knowing it, she had changed my mind. I had spent too many years on the wrong side of the law. I wasn't willing to let revenge take me to the wrong side of the grave. I just had to trust that whoever it was they would get theirs somewhere down the road. I had done enough to Somara and taken enough precious time from her. My focus had to be on bringing a close to the insanity that I had created.

The charge hanging over my head was serious It carried a twenty to thirty year sentence. I wanted a life with Somara and I wanted to have children with her and be able to watch them grow up. For those reasons, I didn't have twenty or thirty years to give away. I was thirty-two years old with a lot of living still ahead of me. I had my degree and the experience of having built a successful business. I took solace in the fact that those things meant I had something to build on later if I indeed ended up serving some time.

The Fed's had seized everything I owned on paper, at least in my name. But you can believe this brother wasn't broke. I had placed a package in a safe deposit box at least a year before my arrest. The safe deposit box was in my mother's name and it had close to three quarters of a million dollars in it. I still had some properties that could be sold off if it had come down to it. Each of them was in Somara's name, including the house she and I lived in. The properties were mostly duplex units, which generated monthly income with a legitimate point of origin. The fact that Somara owned two rental properties several years before she and I met made the following property purchases look less suspect.

I figured the Fed's would be looking at Somara's assets and income as well to determine if the money she paid taxes on, would sustain the purchase of the things that were in her name. Though I wasn't too worried about that since Somara made a comfortable living of her own, and her trust fund continued to legitimize her own financial stability. So I felt the house we lived in and the things I had in her name were safe.

Somara hadn't gotten pregnant since her miscarriage and for the first time, I was glad. I wouldn't have wanted her to be pregnant while I didn't even know if I would be free to spend my life with her or locked away in a prison cell. I tried talking to Somara about the possibility of my having to do some time. Whenever I brought it up, she refused to discuss it. Somara said she was only going to hold on to positive thoughts and she was putting her confidence in God and Maurice. I appreciated her positive attitude and I needed it. Though I had to be realistic and look at both sides of the reality that I was facing.

I sat down and wrote Somara a letter and explained to her about all of my finances, and where the deeds and titles to everything I owned was located. I wanted her to have access to everything. I was still angry with myself for putting her in the crazy situation that I had created. I didn't get out of the game in time, but I had handled my money wisely.

It was a week before my trial was scheduled to begin. I would be lying if I said that I wasn't nervous and even scared about the end results of it all. The thought of spending twenty to thirty years in the penitentiary was definitely enough to break the hardest brother. That made me nervous about walking into the courtroom and watching my future be decided right before my eyes.

Maurice spent a lot of time pouring himself over law books, drug cases that had been appealed, previous decisions handed down by the Supreme Court and every inch of the law he thought would get me off. My brother was ready and I trusted him completely. Whatever he was able to make happen, I knew I would end up better off then if he weren't there with me fighting for my life.

I spent the last few days before my trial started just spending time with Somara doing things I had promised her we would get to. We took a dinner cruise on Lake Michigan, walked down Navy Pier and enjoyed the live entertainment on the waterfront. The midnight picnic in downtown Chicago on the lakefront, which she surprised me with, was very romantic. All simple things that I just hadn't made time to do. Every second that I spent with her made me appreciate her even more. Often when people are confronted with life altering situations they value life so much more. I wasn't any different.

The few days Somara and I spent together before I had to sit in the courtroom felt so good. I remember laying out on the deck in our back yard on pillow soft lawn chairs just talking to her. The sound of her voice and the soft warm touch of her hand on my arm were both relaxing. I watched her look out across the yard at the two squirrels that were chasing each other up and down the tree branch. I thought about how beautiful she was and how soft her lips looked and tasted. She gently squeezed the skin on my arm between her thumb and index finger. I closed my eyes as she continued to squeeze the skin up and down my arm. It was relaxing and I just wanted to enjoy her touching me. For a little while my cares seemed so far away.

The night before my trial started I spent several hours lying in bed next to Somara with the weariness of sleep no where to be found. I considered the path my life had taken, the years that had past, and the promises that had been made and kept. I wished things had turned out differently. When the truth was they hadn't turned out differently because I had done what so many drug-dealing brothers do. I stayed in the game too long.

Chapter 11

As I walked into the courtroom it felt like my body was passing through a thick heavy maze of smoke that was hidden by some hard almost impenetrable wall. With every step, I could feel the heaviness of my feet as I struggled in my mind to put one foot in front of the other. It was almost as if I was going to the guillotine and its sharp blade was the only light shining through the murky haze that seemed to fill the courtroom. The smell in the air was just as thick. The scent was kind of a combination of stale air and a floral air freshener that was unsuccessful in its efforts.

I looked up at the empty judge's bench, then over to the empty area where the jury would be seated. For a second I saw my mother sitting there in one of those empty seats. She was smiling at me. She put her finger up to her mouth as if to say, "Ssshhh don't tell anyone." Then her lips moved as she mouthed, "I love you." Somara squeezed my hand as she was about to take a seat at the end of the isle. It was that sobering moment that ended what felt like a real interaction between my mother and me.

I followed Maurice to the front of the courtroom where we both sat down. I remember the tightness that I felt in my chest when the court bailiff walked into the courtroom and asked everyone to stand. Maurice placed his hand on my shoulder firmly. When I looked at him, he said in a low confident voice, "It will work out." It was like he read my mind and knew I needed to hear him say things would be okay.

My trial started with the prosecuting attorney giving her opening statements. Maurice told me that the state had been very deliberate in their selection of the attorney to prosecute my case. The states weapon of choice was an articulate and attractive woman with smooth chocolate colored skin. She had killer calves and full luscious lips that would make every man on the jury pay attention to every single word that came out of her mouth.

She started her assault with the stern vicious look she gave me while she stood and leaned forward on her fingertips, as she pressed them firmly into the table in front of her. She didn't take her eyes off me until she was half way to the jury box. Then she quickly turned to face the jurors, and with a firm voice, she addressed them.

"Don't be misled by the smooth, handsome, well dressed man that you see before you. Criminals can afford tailors just like Fortune 500 CEO's."

She went on to talk about how she planned to prove that I was guilty of manufacturing and trafficking drugs. She promised to deliver to the jury more than a reasonable doubt of my guilt. She frequently looked over at me with those beautiful but cold hazel eyes of hers, while she talked to the jury. I could only believe that with the look in her eyes, she was promising me a prison sentence. But my attorney had a few choice words of his own to share.

Maurice buttoned his suit jacket as he stood. The brother looked like he had stepped off the cover of G. Q. Magazine. A dark blue tailored suit with faint gray pin stripes hung well on his frame, which couldn't hide the regular upper-body workout regiment Maurice was committed to. He stepped from behind the table where we were sitting. Walking toward the jury, he smiled. When he stood directly in front of them he started painting his verbal portrait of me.

"Ladies and gentlemen of the jury, good morning. Are either of you familiar with my client?" Each juror responded, "No."

"No, you're not familiar with him, because my client, Mr. Johnson, is not the big time drug dealer that you've read headlines about. He's not a long sought after head of a drug cartel. He's not part of a drug war that has cost innocent children their lives because they were caught in rival gunfire while they played on the sidewalk. Mr. Johnson, stand please."

I wasn't sure if I should stand or not. Somehow it seemed to me like that wouldn't be allowed. But I looked right into Maurice's eyes and stood as he had instructed me to.

"Ladies and gentlemen of the jury, you're looking at a man who became the self appointed guardian of his brother when their mother was killed. You're looking at a man who got his brother and himself out of the projects and through college with degrees. A man who mentored two young boys whose father walked out on them. Mr. Johnson taught them how to respect themselves as well as respect women. He encouraged them to work hard in school and set goals for themselves. He wanted those young boys to know that even though they didn't have a father in their lives, they did have a man that was in their corner. That man was Mr. Johnson."

Maurice nodded his head at me to sit down. Everything he said about me was true. He wanted the jury to see me as a person. He wanted them to see me as a man with feelings and some character. He also wanted the expression on my face and my reaction to his words to be genuine. That's why he didn't tell me in advance what he would be saying in is opening statement, or that he would be asking me to stand.

I had never seen my brother in action in a courtroom before that day. But I was beginning to see why he made the big bucks. The boy was cold! He finished his opening statement and took his seat next to me.

During the trial I saw Denise in the courtroom a few times. She and her boys sent me a letter saying that their prayers and support were with me and that I would always have a special place in their hearts. I had come to love those boys of hers, Kyle and Kevin. They were good kids that just needed a chance. I was relieved to know that they weren't upset and disappointed in me because of the charges I was facing. It was then that I knew they loved me too. When you love someone, you show them even more love when they've made a mistake. Because you know it's then that they need to feel your unconditional love the most.

Maurice had done a good job of anticipating how the state would present their case. There was only one thing that took us both by surprise. The prosecuting attorney called Gavin

Andrews as a witness. I wasn't familiar with that name. But when the witness walked into the courtroom, I was definitely familiar with the face. It was "Money" the one person in my organization that I came close to trusting. We called him "Money" but I knew him as Steve Williams. I guess in actuality, I didn't know him at all.

Gavin Andrews walked up the aisle and then past the table I was sitting at. He never looked my way once. He took the witness stand, swore to tell the truth, and sat down as he kept his eyes fixed straight ahead of him. Gavin Andrews, or whoever the hell he was, sat there dressed in an expensive suit and wearing more than once piece of pricey jewelry All of which I was sure that I had funded since he worked for me. I paid him more money in a year than most doctors' make in two years.

I didn't have to wonder any longer about who was the traitor in my camp. He was sitting right in front of me. Gavin played his role well. He would not have been one of the first people I considered in my efforts to hunt down the dog that took my money and then dared to bite my hand.

The prosecuting attorney stood in front of Gavin and threw question after question at him. He told her that he had worked for me several years. He painted a picture of me being this ruthless New Jack City type of drug lord. He told the court that the lieutenants who worked for me would just as well deliver a nine millimeter bullet to someone's head as deliver a bag of crack to a regular customer. An order was given to him to take out a guy who had stolen a large amount of cocaine, cocaine that was worth about $100,000 dollars. I was the person that had given the order. At least that was what Gavin told the court. When asked if he had indeed killed the man, Gavin said he told me that he did and I wasn't concerned with proof because he was able to recover the value of the product in cash.

I wasn't a saint but I definitely wasn't the demon he was making me out to be. I couldn't believe this man was just out and out lying and with so much depth. Now I was supposed to be guilty of attempting to contract a murder too.

The state must have really offered him a good deal for the pack of lies that he sold them. I didn't expect that he would be serving a day behind bars. The jurors sure did look attentive throughout his verbal assault of me. Maurice cast a significant amount of doubt on his credibility, after the questions that he put to Gavin uncovered his arrest record for assault, possession of narcotics, and the four years he served for manslaughter. After that he wasn't looking much like the person to be pointing fingers.

Gavin had set me up like he was out for revenge. Revenge for what I couldn't possibly think of. I had been good to him and I definitely took him up the climb to money with me. When my spot got robbed and I put the word on the street that I wanted my money back, Gavin kept his promise. He had my money back in my hands and much quicker than I had expected.

That very money was the key to his setting me up. The bag the money was in had a voice activated recorder hidden in it. That made it possible for our conversation to be recorded when he returned the money to me. Of course, the money was marked also. I didn't really say anything that tied me to the specific things in my indictment. But the recording put me in the same room with Gavin and the drug money that had been marked by the Fed's and returned to me as my own. It was returned by "Money." A man who admitted to playing a significant role in the narcotics crimes that I was on trial for.

It was the defense's turn to present our case. Maurice presented character witnesses and financial records to substantiate the income generated from my business and real estate holdings. As for the money the Fed's bugged, Maurice argued that I never admitted to the money being drug money when it was returned to me. I didn't engage in a conversation about a Kilo of cocaine that Gavin had tried to bate me into.

It was definitely a plus that the $100,000 could have easily been generated from my consulting business, based on my tax records.

It was finally time for closing arguments. The courtroom was full but silent. I knew the silence wouldn't last long. As the attractive prosecutor stood, I looked back at Somara. She smiled and I mouthed to her, "I Love you." Looking into her eyes for just those few seconds hurt my heart. I could see her pain and her fear. I turned my attention to the front of the courtroom. I'm sure that I appeared to be listening to both closing arguments. I tried to, but my mind kept going back in time.

I thought about Maurice and me growing up and all the fun we had as kids. We were always close, even though I was four years older than him. He never gave my mother any trouble. If my mother had to tell either of us to do something twice, it would have been me. We were both pretty good kids though. My mother loved us so much. I thought about her also that day. Somehow I felt her presence and the warm embrace of her love. I can't explain it, but I felt like I was wrapped up in one of those big hugs she would give us when we came home from school. She always loved us no matter what we did and I knew at that moment she loved me no matter what I had done.

I thought back to the day that I first saw Somara running across the street in that gorgeous red dress. I regretted her having to be in the courtroom with me that day. However, I didn't regret her being in my life. She had taken me from just existing to living. I was determined that I couldn't let anything or anyone take her away from me. That meant I would have to find a way for us to stay together even if we had to be apart.

The closing arguments were finished. The judge gave the jury their instructions and dismissed them to decide my fate. The sound of the judge's gavel made me think of a cell door slamming closed behind me. Everyone in the courtroom stood as the judge made his exit. I stood their wondering if I would be able to walk out that courtroom a free man.

We left the courtroom with Maurice in silence. It was late so the verdict wouldn't come back that day. The three of us went to dinner. Surprisingly, I laughed and had a good time. The two people that I loved most in the world loved me for who I was and didn't turn against me for what I had done. For that I was thankful.

I found myself dusting off my praying skills that night. I hadn't talked to the man upstairs much after my mother died, though I had prayed when I got the call about Maurice being in a car accident. That night, I found myself in prayer again, but not for me, for Somara and Maurice. I needed God to take care of Somara and not let Maurice's defense of me damage his career.

Chapter 12

I watched the sun peak through the scattered clouds of early morning. The leaves were starting to turn green. The birds were waking up the neighborhood with the lively songs of spring. It was time for new beginnings. Just not for me. I still had some old business to finish. When Somara woke up I had already been awake for an hour. I expected the call to come telling us that the jury had come in. I wasn't wrong. Maurice got the call shortly after we had all eaten breakfast.

As I walked up the steps to the courthouse, I counted each one wondering how many years the judge would sentence me to if I was found guilty. I was back in front of the judge's bench and for some reason hoping nobody had pissed him off. I took a deep breath as the jury filed into the courtroom. The judge's voice was stern when he asked the jury if they had reached a verdict. I watched the jury foreman's lips move when he answered the judge. I didn't want to hear the words that came out of his mouth. Unfortunately, I couldn't prevent anything that happened next.

The judge's strong voice said, "Will the defendant please rise." Maurice and I stood. I knew he was just as nervous as I was because the tip of his noise was sweating. That was always a giveaway for Maurice. I stood there wishing that I could just stop time and change the past. The jury foreman stood slowly as if it were a difficult task for him to stand. It was almost like I was watching him move in slow motion. He must have had a bad knee or bad back. The judge asked him for the verdict. He looked down at the small piece of paper in his hand as if he had to remind himself of what was on it. However, his voice was clear and firm when it rang out with the word, "Guilty."

I had been found guilty of manufacturing and trafficking narcotics with the intent to sell. The guilty verdict didn't really surprise me. I wasn't guilty of everything the prosecution put before the jury, but my hands were dirty. I heard the sorrow in Somara's voice behind me when she cried out, "Oh my God." I didn't turn to her because I couldn't bare to see her tears. "Sentencing will take place in two weeks." Those were the last words the judge said before the sound of his gavel let me know I wasn't dreaming. Maurice had prepared me for the possibility of a guilty verdict. He also said he had planned an appeal and had been working on some aspects of what it would consist of already. That was just like Maurice to be prepared for anything.

I thanked my brother for all the time and effort he had put into my defense. We hugged and he told me he was working on something related to my case that might work in our favor somewhere down the line. He needed to check on a few things and he would catch up with me later. I finally had to turn around and face the sadness in Somara's eyes. My heart broke as I saw the tears that she desperately hurried to wipe away.

The few steps I took to reach her felt heavy like there was cement in my shoes. I held her tightly in my arms as she sobbed on my shoulder. Her tears were heavy to me, mostly because I was the reason for the sorrow she was being tormented by.

The court bailiff had to ask Somara and me to leave the courtroom. We hadn't noticed that everyone else had already cleared out. We walked out of the courthouse and quickly became a part of the crowd of people that hurried through downtown Chicago. Only the pace of our steps was much slower than the people that surrounded us that we didn't really even notice anyway.

The drive home was pretty quiet. I guess we were both lost in our own thoughts about how the sentencing would go and what would follow that. Our lives were about to change, and I was definitely thinking that I had no control of that. Somehow I had driven home with no thought of one corner I turned or even one stoplight that required me to sit still in time. As I opened the car door for Somara, I wished I could have been opening the door to a new life that didn't have any of the drama that she and I had just gone through. But before the evening had past, I promised her that day would come.

The evening consisted of precious time spent with the woman that I was about to miss more than I could even imagine. We didn't eat dinner; we did however finish what we started. We made love in each of the rooms that were left untouched on Christmas day when I took her to our house for the first time.

The red dress Somara wore the first day that I saw her was beautiful and had embedded a memory in my mind that I would never be able to let go of. I asked Somara to always keep that dress in her closet. She did me one better. I had gone downstairs to make sure the house was locked up. When I got back upstairs, she was standing in our bedroom, wearing that red dress with nothing on underneath. She gave me a long sensuous kiss as I lifted her up and wrapped my arms around her. Then she led me out onto the deck at the back of our house. It overlooked the heated swimming pool and manicured lawn.

Every curve of her luscious body was calling my name. I watched her move in the moonlight with a rhythm that made me crave her. The seductive motion of her hips took me back to the first time we made love. Her nipples stood at attention as the chill of the night air breezed through the almost sheer material of her dress and it made my body ache for her. I put both my hands around her small waist. I pressed my weight in against her and gently leaned her body into the railing. Kissing the back of her neck, I slowly entered her body.

She gasped lightly and I felt the breath she took as her shoulders raised up and pressed into my chest when she inhaled. It was almost impossible for me to not release my love inside of her the moment we became one. But I wanted to be sure she felt pleasure with every stroke and that she had as much of me as she needed.

I matched the rhythm of my strokes with her body as she moved with me. I felt the warm wet juices inside of her embrace me. Moments later we met each other's desperate need to be one even if only for a brief moment in time. After about twenty minutes of cuddling and talking, we showered together which we hadn't done in a long time. She soon fell asleep in my arms and seemed to rest peacefully. However, sleep eluded me for hours. I lay there thinking back over my life and reliving all the major disasters and triumphs I had experienced. Sleep didn't come until I looked up in the corner of the ceiling and I could faintly see the image of my mother's face. She smiled at me and said, "Sleep now son. I love you!"

Two weeks passed by quickly and the day of reckoning came sooner than I was ready for. I took my time getting dressed that morning. It would be the last time I stood next to Somara in our bathroom and watched her fuss over how to wear her hair, at least the last time for a while. The question that troubled my heart that morning, was just how long would that time be?

Somara and I walked up the steps to the courthouse like we had unfortunately, done before. Maurice was already inside waiting for us. I was hoping to see my mother's face in the juror's stand again. When I stepped onto the elevator there she was smiling at me. When I was six, I broke the femur bone in my thigh and was in traction for three weeks. My mother was there in the hospital sitting right next to my bed. She told me then that she would always be with me and she would never leave me. My mother always kept her promises.

The inside of the court room looked just like we left it two weeks prior; except this time there wasn't an audience in the courtroom and there wasn't a jury. Maurice stood at the front of the courtroom waiting for me to take my place at the table next to him. I did, and he gave me an envelope and told me to open it later. I started to ask him what was in the envelope but he took the envelope from my hand and put it in the inside pocket of my suit jacket.

The court bailiff's stern voice commanded us to stand as the judge took his place on the bench. The few moments of silence before the judge spoke were harsh, because it made me think of the silence I expected to have in my prison cell in the middle of the night. I wouldn't have Somara's sexy voice whispering in my ear at night as she often did before we fell asleep.

The judge directed me to stand. Maurice stood with me as I looked directly at the judge. The next few minutes went by quickly.

"Does the defendant have anything to say before I impose sentence upon him?"

My response was brief but sincere; "I appreciate the tremendous diligence on the part of my attorney in his development of my defense. I sincerely regret the hurt and pain this situation has brought to those that love me. Thank you!"

The crushing blow that followed my addressing the judge was expected, although there was no way to be prepared for it.

"This court sentences you to one hundred and twenty months, a term of ten years, to be served in the Federal Bureau of prisons. The defendant will be immediately taken into custody by the U.S. Marshall's Service."

I turned to Somara and told her that I loved her. As I was escorted through a side door of the courtroom, my brother said to me, in a firm and confident voice, "Hold tight. It's not over yet!" I was hustled into a police van and rode for about two and a half hours before I reached The Federal Correctional Institution in Pekin IL, a medium security facility that housed almost twelve hundred men and my new place of residence.

Chapter 13

"A young Black attorney was held at gunpoint in broad daylight in downtown Chicago. Some people appeared to hurry past without even realizing a man was being robbed, while two other courageous men attempted to help him. Their selfless efforts ended with one of the men being shot fatally three times in the chest. The robber then turned the gun on the attorney and with one shot to the head his life ended also."

"The screams of hysteria rang out loudly from the voices of people running to take cover. The assailant was described as a six-foot African American man weighing about two hundred and twenty five pounds. He has a mustache and a tattoo of a teardrop underneath his left eye. He was reported to be wearing black jeans, a white T-shirt and a blue hooded jacket. Anyone with information related to this robbery that resulted in two senseless killings is urged to please contact your local authorities."

Those were the words printed on the page of a Chicago newspaper the day after Maurice was killed. He left the courthouse after I had been taken into custody when my sentencing was over. I'm sure he walked out of the building sorrowful about the turn of events in my life. Now I'm sorrowful that my little brother's life is over.

A guard came to my cell and told me the Chaplin wanted to see me. That made me nervous because I didn't know what to expect. He was direct. "I'm sorry to have to tell you that your brother has been killed." I fell to my knees and screamed out in pain. My heart literally hurt. I thought I was having a heart attack. I couldn't believe it. Not my brother. He was all the family that I had left. I sobbed like a child. The Chaplin embraced me and said, "Let it go son. Our tears have a healing power and God is able in all things. He, and He alone, can give you peace in this your time of desperate sorrow."

When I was able to compose myself, the Chaplin gave me the details of how Maurice was killed. He let me use the phone in his office to call Somara. I was thankful that he stepped outside the door and gave me a little privacy. Somara answered the phone on the first ring.

"Somara baby, it's me."

"Malcolm, hello sweetheart. I've been waiting for your call. I don't know what to say. You know I loved Maurice. He was an absolutely wonderful man."

"Thank you baby! He thought you were the sweetest woman he'd ever met. He told me once that if I was ever foolish enough to let you go, he might have to see just how tight his game was." We both laughed at the same time. It felt good to laugh and the sound of Somara's laughter was a little shred of pleasure that I could hold on to.

"Baby, I hate to ask you but..."

"You don't have to ask me. I've already made some calls. I'll take care of the funeral arrangements. I booked a flight to Atlanta so I can go through his apartment and pack up his personal things, which I'll bring home and store away for you to go through once you're back. I called the law firm that he had worked for to let them know about Maurice's death. I got the name and phone number of a few people that he was close to there. So I will be contacting them. I thought maybe I could get someone to auction off the furniture in his apartment and give the proceeds to a homeless shelter, unless you want me to do something different."

"I love you girl! You are so good to me. Thank you for loving me. It feels inadequate to say that I appreciate you and all the support that you constantly give me. But I do appreciate you baby more than I can tell you."

"I love you sweetheart! I will always be here for you. There is no way that I couldn't. Let the Chaplin know to give me a call and I will work with him to make the arrangements to get you home for the funeral."

"I love you baby! I'll have the Chaplin call you and I'll call you again as soon as I can." That conversation was painful for me. Having to discuss the need to make funeral arrangements for my brother was not something I expected to have to do.

When I closed my eyes that night, I thought about mama and Maurice being happy to see each other again. They had to be up there together with the Lord. They were both watching over me.

Five days later I was on the outside of the prison walls, but I wasn't free. I was allowed to attend my brother's funeral and for that short time I didn't even have on handcuffs.

Looking around the church, I recognized a lot of guys Maurice and I went to school with. Even some of my friends were there. Some the years had been kind to and others not so much. Mrs. Hayes wrapped her big arms around me tightly like she used to do when Maurice and I would stop by her house on the way home from school. She and mama kept our butts in line. If Mrs. Hayes saw us doing anything we had no business doing, she would threaten us with a switch. She was from Arkansas and she had that "I mean what I say" mentality. By the time we got home mama would have her belt already drawn back over her shoulder and ready to do what Mrs. Hayes had only threatened to do.

Somara was standing right behind Mrs. Hayes as she told me how sorry she was about Maurice. I noticed her shifting her weight from one foot to the other as her full red lips mouthed, "I love you." I imagine that she was ready for Mrs. Hayes to take her seat. Once Somara was in my arms, I didn't want to let her go. Her body felt so good against mine. I kissed her gently on the lips and we walked up to the front row and sat down. The funeral was held at the same church as my mother's funeral.

The church was full. The funeral director had to bring in folding chairs to accommodate more people as they continued to pour in. The walls served as leaning post for others. I sat through the service thinking about all the years that Maurice and I had together as boys growing up. You hear people say, "Time is short, live life every day to it's fullest, and tell those you cherish that you love them." Those words rang out loudly in my head that day.

When the time came to view the body, I couldn't hold my tears back any longer. I stood looking into his casket thinking how much I hated that his body would soon be lowered into the cold hard ground. I looked at him for the last time and before I walked away, I hoped that he could hear me say, "I love you man. You were your 'Brother's Keeper' too. Give mama my love."

Chapter 14

Seventeen days and sixteen hours after I had been taken into custody by U.S. Marshalls and transported to prison, I finally heard my name for mail call. It was the first mail I had received since being incarcerated. I guess it took awhile for the mail to track down a person when they're new to the penal system. I expected to see an envelope with Somara's name on it, I didn't expect the yellow envelope that had the words "Legal Papers" stamped across the front of it.

I walked back to my cell inhaling the soft sweet smell of Somara's perfume which she had laced her letter with. My mind drifted back to us making love on the deck. I could almost feel her smooth skin and the sexy red dress that gently hugged her body while we made love. I put my daydream on pause once I reached my cell. Although, I was anxious to read Somara's letter, I decided to satisfy my curiosity about what was in the yellow envelope first.

I sat down on my bunk and tore into the unexpected package. It held indictment papers and the discovery documents detailing factual findings of my case. Also inside were my trial transcripts, the witness list and the letter Maurice had placed inside my jacket pocket the day I was sentenced. With Maurice's death, the funeral, and just grieving the loss of my brother, I had forgotten all about the letter. He was gone and I was about to read something he had given me the same day he died. That felt really strange.

Malcolm,

I regret deeply that I had to write this letter. Please know that I did absolutely my very best in defending you. Although you're serving time, it's not over yet. I've contacted a friend of mine in the justice department. He's going to go over every piece of evidence, the court transcripts and an article of law that I think might help in getting an appeal heard or your sentence reduced. I promise you that I will look out for Somara and I'll be there to visit you on a regular basis. I know soo many brothers unfortunately do their time alone. But know and believe, I'm there with you in thought and concern. Just like mama, I'll never leave you. You can count on me until the day I die. I love you man and I got you every step of the way!
Love Maurice

I was looking at the words on the page of the letter but I could hear Maurice's voice say every word in my ear. The day I was sentenced, I thought going to prison was the worst thing that could happen to me. When you're going through something difficult, it's hard to remember that things could be worse. Worse was starring me right in the face and I couldn't stand the sight of it. Maurice was dead and I was looking at his last words to me written down on a piece of paper.

The first six months of my sentence were hard as hell. Every move I made from the time I was told to get up in the morning, until the time I was told to go to bed at night was dictated to me. The only thing I had control over was my thoughts. That definitely took some time to swallow.

Mail call was really the only resemblance of the world outside of the bars that confined me. The time it took for me to read Somara's letters allowed me a life beyond my cell. Sometimes I would read the same letter from her three or four times a day. I can't imagine how some brothers serve time and never get any mail or a visit. That is too cruel.

I sold drugs to keep Maurice and me with money in our pockets and out of the gangs. Those same drugs ended me up in prison trying hard not to end up on the wrong side of some prison gang. Prison life is hard to say the least. It's almost like you're not alive. Your body is lifeless as you lie in your bunk looking up at the ceiling and the air around you is stale. Lying there I often felt like I was lying in a casket.

One of the biggest pass times in prison is listening to the stories people tell about why their serving time and the crazy heartless stuff some of them did. My cellmate was serving twenty-five years for bank robbery. His cousin was in a different prison serving a double life sentence for killing seven people. He caught his wife in bed with his brother. The next day she filed for divorce and went to the bank and cleaned out the entire $75,000 from their joint bank account. When he found out, he went home and shot his wife, their three kids and cut the dog's throat. Then he drove across town and shot his wife's mother, her brother and the six year old little girl the mother was babysitting.

Thank God Somara visited me at least twice a month and I got to talk to her on a regular basis. Her visits and my calls to her offered me an escape from the insanity of prison. Though there was a period of time when I was a little concerned. She still sounded like she was glad to talk to me each time I called but something wasn't right. Our conversations were shorter. She complained about being tired and not having any energy. I wished that I were there with her making sure that she was okay. Over the next thirty days, there were a few times that I called her and I wasn't able to catch her. A couple of months later, I called her every night for two weeks and she never answered the phone one time.

For a while I thought that she must have been laying it out for another brother. That was the only thing I could think of. How could I blame her? It was my fault that I was behind bars and had left her out there without me. I tried to put the thought out of my mind that she might not stay faithful to me. Even if she gave her body to somebody else, I didn't believe she'd give her heart to somebody else. But like so many brothers, I selfishly wanted her to completely stay true to me.

Another day had passed and I tried again to call Somara. With every ring my heart was beating faster. Then finally she answered the phone. I asked her why I hadn't been able to get in touch with her. What was going on and was she all right. Her voice was soft but her sad tone worried me.

She said, "Baby, I'm okay. I really don't want to go into it right now. I know you have a lot of questions, but for now, just let it go, okay."

I couldn't believe what I was hearing. I said to her in a harsh voice, "Just let it go. Come on now. Baby you have to tell me something." As soon as the words left my mouth she started to cry. I couldn't console her. I decided to let it go if that would stop her tears. But in my heart, I felt like something bad was going on, or had already happened, and there was nothing that I could do to help her.

Things went back to normal with us talking on the phone on a regular basis. Though something definitely wasn't normal in the background of our conversations. Frequently when I would talk with Somara I could hear a baby in the background. I panicked the first time I heard the baby crying. She quickly calmed my fears by telling me that her girlfriend, Cynthia, who I knew, had given birth to her third child. Children and Family Services had taken her other two children away from her because of neglect. Somara told me she was babysitting for Cynthia so she could work a third shift job. That didn't seem odd to me since Somara was always trying to help someone. I also thought the company of a child would be good for Somara.

Two years passed and I was still behind bars and this child was still a part of Somara's life. She laughed a lot and I could hear the happiness in her voice when she talked about the little boy. I asked about Cynthia and Somara told me she had been arrested for writing bad checks. That was why the little boy, she said his name was David, was spending more and more time with her. She was happy about having him in her life. So, I had to be happy for her.

Besides Somara, Denise and her boys, I never got any mail. Somara was the only person that ever came to see me. When I read her letter telling me that she would be visiting me in a few days, I was excited.

I expected to see Somara in the visiting room. I didn't expect to see David sitting next to her. The black denim jeans that hugged her hips looked just as good as the black knit sweater she wore that wrapped itself around her still enticing plump breast. Man, she looked too good. Though I was puzzled why she had brought David with her, I was happy to see her standing there. I walked over and hugged her while I looked down at the little boy. She quickly started to explain.

"Baby, I didn't tell you that I was bringing David because I wanted to discuss something with you in person. Just hear me out. I miss you more than I can say. Sleeping alone at night and walking around that big house by myself is killing me inside. The ache I felt in my heart the day you were sentenced, and I went home without you, I still feel every single day of my life. Not having you there with me, it's just too hard for me to take."

"I have a chance to adopt David. Cheryl wants me to give him something that she can't, a stable home. You know how much I wanted us to have children together. After the miscarriage, I hoped every month that I would be able to say to you 'I'm pregnant.' You know just like I do, that never happened. I want us to be a family. We can be that, the three of us. I need you to hear my heart. Baby let me have this, please!"

I saw apprehension in her eyes. She must have been worried about what my response would be. I kissed her on the cheek and said; "I know this has been hard for you. My heart breaks every night right along with yours. Sleep doesn't come easy to me. I think about things we've done together, our first date, and so many times that you've made me smile. At some point, eventually, I fall asleep. I can only imagine how you feel when you lie down at night alone in our bed."

"This is definitely not how I expected our family to start. But how can I say no." I watched the tears well up in her eyes as I was talking to her. I couldn't ignore the rise and fall of her chest while she breathed a little uneasy and wiped the tears from her eyes. I spent the rest of the visit enjoying the happiness that I saw in Somara's face and wondering how this would all work out once I got home.

Omar was a couple of cells down from me. Occasionally I would talk to him about how bad I felt that Somara was out there alone and how much she meant to me. I told him about Somara's visit and that she planned on adopting David. I remember him telling me that I wasn't being realistic. He said for me to think a fine woman like Somara would keep herself on hold for me while I did my time in prison, just didn't make a lot of sense.

I put my hands around his throat when he said I was a fool not to see the little boy was Somara's and his daddy was the man she was laying it out for. I don't know if I was angry because of what he said or because that was what I really thought myself. Either way, I didn't talk to Omar anymore after that day. I decided to go right on trusting what Somara had told me about David. It was the only way I could get through each day.

Chapter 15

One thousand two hundred and seventy seven days and nights had been spent behind bars and I was finally going home. I spent the last night playing chess and talking about women with a few of the guys on my tier. Most of them had several years left to serve, which made them envious of me.

Maurice was still impacting my life even beyond the grave. Because of him I was going home long before my prison sentence was over. The paperwork that he had sent to his friend Nathaniel, in the justice department, had been right on the money. Three months earlier, Nathaniel had come to visit me and explained the paper work Maurice had forwarded to him even before my trial ended. Maurice had requested him to review the trial details and transcripts. Maurice wanted him to challenge the sufficiency of the evidence related to the audio conversation between Money and me when he returned the cash to me.

The two-week time frame between my being found guilty and sentenced, Maurice spent doing research for my appeal. He told me that he was working on something he thought might get my conviction over turned. I wanted to know the details but he said he needed to check out a couple of things first. He did say that it had something to do with pending legislature related to drug convictions. Maurice never got to tell me the details.

Instead, it was Nathaniel telling me about the changes in the law since my conviction. State legislature had imposed changes that would make about 900 prisoners with drug related charges eligible for re-sentencing under the Drug Law Reform Act. The law provided for determinate sentencing for felony drug offenders and permitted people who were convicted under the old law to apply for re-sentencing.

Nathaniel put the process in motion. Based on the new law, I would have only been sentenced to three years. I had already served three years and two months when Nathaniel came to me. That, along with a couple of other errors in the trial process, was the key to opening my cell door. It took the next three months to get all the paper work filed and processed with the courts. I was finally going home.

I thought back to what Maurice said to me, as I was lead out of the courtroom by Federal Marshalls. "Hold tight. It's not over yet!"

Once Maurice was killed, I never gave those words another thought. But there I was about to walk out of prison seven and a half years early.

When I walked through the big electrical gate, as it slowly opened, I looked up into the watchtower at the guards armed with automatic assault weapons. I took the last step through the gate and the air on the other side of the gate even smelled different. As I reclaimed my freedom, it almost felt like I had been out of the country for the last three and a half years. Shielding my eyes from the sun with my hand, I could see Somara leaning against her car. There was my baby looking just as fine as ever.

Watching her run toward me and then feeling her firm body pressed up against mine was like a scene you see in a movie. I think we must have kissed for at least five minutes. I looked at her and I couldn't say anything. I was full inside and so happy to see her. I kissed her again and hugged her tightly. When I finally let her go, we both said, "I love you" at the same time.

The drive home was filled with conversation about all the time we had missed with each other. We both promised not to let anything ever again keep us away from each other. I felt a little nervous about going home to a child that I hadn't left there. For Somara's sake, I had a made up mind to make it work.

I asked Somara where David was. She told me he was spending the night with one of his little friends from school. She wanted us to enjoy some private time together.

David was a handsome little two and a half year old boy. Somara sent me pictures of him at least every couple of months. She made sure that every birthday and holiday I got to see what was going on with him. That helped me to feel like I wasn't going home to a total stranger. But there was definitely some discomfort on my part.

When we got home, I told Somara to go on into the house and I'd be in shortly. I'm not sure why, but for some reason, I just wasn't ready to walk into that house. I got out of the car and walked around to the back yard. The water in the pool was clean and I could see down to the bottom. The flowers and the healthy looking lawn were both soaking up the water from the sprinklers. Everything outside of the house looked the same. Somara must have had a lawn service taking care of things. The shinny gloss on the deck made me think it had been recently treated.

Things looked good and I should have felt good. In truth, my homecoming was bitter sweet. Maurice should have been there standing next to Somara when I walked through that prison gate. I didn't see him there and I wouldn't be seeing him ever again.

Somara said that she called my name a couple of times before I noticed that she was standing on the deck. She was waiting for me to come into the house. I told her that I was thinking about Maurice and how much I missed him. Although I was a little sad, I didn't want Somara to feel like I wasn't happy to be home with her.

Leaving thoughts of Maurice behind me for the moment, I walked back around to the front of the house. The door was still standing open. When I got a few steps away from the front door, I thought I heard my mother's voice behind me. I looked back over my shoulder. Of course, she wasn't there. When I turned around to walk up the steps, I saw her smiling face in the doorway. It was only for a second. But I had to think she was smiling because she and Maurice were together and I had come home.

A few things inside the house were different. Somara had bought some new art and the leather chaise that she and I had talked about getting for the living room. Home didn't feel like home. Maybe I just needed a couple of days to get comfortable.

My baby threw down in the kitchen for a brother's home coming. Fried chicken, sweet potatoes, collard greens and skillet-fried corn bread, woke up my taste buds. Everything was homemade. I don't know where Somara learned how to cook, but she didn't short stop at all. I hadn't eaten food that was edible in so long that I forgot how good food can taste. I thought I didn't want dessert until she pulled a peach cobbler out of the oven. I ate two bowls of that and I wasn't any good for the rest of the evening. I laid across the bed to let my food settle. When I woke up, it was three in the morning and Somara was lying next to me. I had fallen a sleep fully dressed.

I woke up horny as hell. I definitely didn't mean to fall asleep without making love to the gorgeous woman who had stood by my side. I made it up to her shortly before the sun rose. She had never peaked multiple times before. That night, I counted at least three. To be truthful, when she fell back to sleep, I still hadn't had enough of her.

Three nights of feeling Somara's soft body next to mine was definitely making home feel like home again. I had promised David I would help him break in his new baseball glove on Saturday. That meant sleeping in wasn't going to happen because he was already knocking on our bedroom door.

"Daddy, you got to get up. I got my glove. You ready?" He sounded so cute. I was still getting use to being called "daddy." But I liked it and Somara knew it. She said my eyes smiled every time David called me that. As if she could talk. The bond between her and David was definitely that of a mother and her child. The special connection between them was obvious. It was like she had been the only mother that he had ever known.

Some old doubt started to raise its ugly head again. Was he really hers? Maybe she just couldn't stand being lonely all that time I was away and ended up pregnant. It was obvious she loved David. A mother's love is strong. I figured it was just the strength of that love I was seeing in their relationship. So I just put the doubt out of my mind.

David and I hadn't been outside long before I noticed my neighbor, Russ, who lived two houses down on the other side of the street. He was standing in his yard talking to another man and pointing in my direction. I took a second and looked around to see whom he might have been pointing at. I didn't see any other neighbors out in their yard. I yelled down the street, "Good Morning." I didn't get the response I expected. My neighbor looked right at me, turned his head abruptly, and walked into his garage with the other man following behind him. He and I had been friendly in the past. We'd talked about the Chicago Bears chances in the super bowl. He had even cleared snow from my driveway a couple of times.

I went back to playing ball with David but I didn't stop thinking about what had just happened. Russ hadn't given me any reason in the past to think that he had an issue with me. When Somara and I moved into the neighborhood, he and his wife were the first people to stop by and introduce themselves. I considered walking across the street to talk with him. Then I decided to just let it go. He had someone at his house and I didn't want to intrude.

I had been home a couple of weeks and I wanted to stop by and see Denise and her boys. Somara suggested that she and David go along and we could all go to the arcades and then take the kids out for pizza. It felt good to introduce David to them as my son. I was glad to see Kevin and Kyle again. They had grown a lot and were about nine and eleven years old then.

They got along well with David and treated him like a little brother. Everybody seemed to have a good time. The ride home was quiet. David had fallen asleep and Somara was on her way as well with her head resting on my shoulder.

As I turned onto our street, I noticed Russ unloading something from the back of his Suburban. I pulled into the driveway and parked. After I walked Somara and David into the house, I started out across the street. I thought I'd help Russ unload his Suburban and that would give me a chance to make sure things with us were cool. The exchange of words between us surprised me. But I remember them clearly.

"Hey, Russ. You need a hand?"

"No thanks, Malcolm. I got it."

"It's not a problem man. I'd be happy to lift a few pounds. I can use the workout."

"I said I got it." His tone was firm and abrupt.

I tried to stay calm as I said, "What's up Russ? You ignored me when I spoke to you the other day out in the yard, and your attitude today isn't any better. Are you pissed with me about something?"

He stopped unloading his truck and made eye-to-eye contact with me when he responded, "Look, I don't want to make this thing ugly. So, just stay on your side of the street and I'll stay on mine."

I was sure he could hear the agitation in my voice when I told him, "If you have a issue with me, be man enough to tell me what it is. We've been cool since I bought my house on this street. So, what's up? All of a sudden, we're not cool?"

Quickly, he responded, "A house you probably bought with drug money. That's not the kind of man I want to be cool with. Or should I say, not the kind of brother, I want to be cool with."

Without thinking, I hurled my sincere response at him as I moved closer to him, almost two inches from his face, "Oh, so now I am the kind of brother that the white boy doesn't want to be cool with. Let me clear something up for you Russ. I had a thriving consulting firm that made more than enough money for me to buy my house. So I didn't need drug money to become a homeowner. I don't remember seeing your face in the courtroom. All you know about my case is what you read in the paper. So if that's how you want to play it, that works for me."

Just telling the story makes me feel the same anger that I felt that day. I was seething mad as I walked back across the street. Russ's face was beet red. I don't know if he was angry or scared. I didn't care which one. Our confrontation made me wonder if the other folks in the neighborhood felt the same way. I hoped not but I definitely wasn't about to lose any sleep over it. I went into my house, closed my door, and ate dinner with my family.

Chapter 16

Twelve kids, balloons, noise makers, cake and ice-cream, and a grill filled with hamburgers and hot dogs, had finally run its course and the last kid had been picked up. David was almost as tired as Somara and I. So I guess that meant his birthday party was a success. The party was lively from beginning to end. Once David blew out the four candles on the top of his cake, the party was off to the races. Except for the little chunky boy that was in David's class who decided to entertain the other kids by swallowing a goldfish, everything went as planned.

I had been home a little over a year. Slowly my consulting business was on the path to being revived. David and I had built a strong bond. I had a son who loved me and I had not only learned to love him but he felt like mine. David's birthday party really made me feel like a dad. My dad missed my growing up by choice, and by choice, I planned to be there for David. He was a handsome little boy with a smooth medium brown complexion and big brown eyes. He got his soft curly hair from his mother. David had a cucumber shaped birthmark on his arm that he would ask me about at least every few months. He always wanted to know why it was there and if it would every go away. He was my inquisitive little man.

Somara and I were still trying to have a child of our own. We thought we were expecting a couple of months after I got home. Somara was five days late for her cycle. We eagerly went out and got a pregnancy test. Looking down at the minus sign on the stick that indicated she wasn't pregnant did more than hurt. I looked into her eyes and all I could say was "I'm sorry baby. I love you so much!" She kissed me and let the weight of her disappointment and body fall into my arms.

I wanted to ignore the ringing phone but Somara said, "David is at school. It could be anything. We'd better answer it." I released my hold on her and she hurried to the phone. We were both about to leave the house for work. I fixed Somara a cup of hot tea to take with her on her drive. I walked back into the living room and she was still on the phone. She held her hand over her chest. Her eyebrows were raised as she squinted her eyes. I hurried over to her and took her hand from her chest and held it tightly. I didn't know what was going on but it looked serious. I tried to ask her what was wrong. But she motioned for me to wait.

A couple of minutes later, she hung the phone up, dropped to her knees and broke down in tears. Nervously, I continued to ask, "Baby, what's wrong? What is it?" She said something but I couldn't understand her through the tears and her labored breathing. I thought she was about to hyperventilate. I took her face in my hands and kissed her gently. I remember saying to her, "Baby, I got you. Tell me what's wrong. Please, tell me what it is."

I was scared and didn't know what to expect, but I waited until she was ready to talk. Ten minutes passed like ten hours. What she finally said blew me away, "Don't hate me. I didn't know what else to do. You were in prison and I was afraid if I told you, you might try to do something crazy. I just didn't know what to think. I wanted you to be able to just focus on doing your time."

"What in the hell are you talking about?" I said quickly with a harsh tone. As soon as the words left my mouth, I wanted to take them back. I just didn't talk to Somara like that. I was frustrated and I wanted her to just say it. What ever it was. At least that was what I thought. Until she said to me, "I was raped and David is my child."

I took a deep breath and swallowed hard. I was thinking that couldn't be true because she told me he was Cheryl's son. It was like she read my mind when she said, "I know I told you he was Cheryl's son. That's not true. He's really mine."

My words and the anger in my voice rang out loudly and all I could say was, "You lied! All this time and you were lying! Raped and you didn't tell me." I know it was selfish and insensitive but I had to get out of there. I just couldn't look at her. I don't know if I was angry with her for not telling me or angry with myself because I wasn't there for her.

I drove for two hours with no destination in mind. I put my foot on the brakes when I saw a red light and I hit the gas pedal when the traffic light was green. By the time I pulled up in the driveway, I wasn't angry with Somara anymore and I was ashamed of how I had treated her. She had been raped and I showed her no concern at all.

I called Somara's name as I walked through the front door. The house was quiet and she didn't respond. I called out to her again with still no response. Her car was in the driveway. So I was pretty sure she was home. I walked up stairs to our bedroom. There she was, asleep. I laid down with her and kissed the back of her neck. I pulled her close to me. When she turned to look at me, I could see that her eyes were red and puffy from crying. I asked her to forgive me for being such a jerk and totally selfish.

I still saw the hurt in her eyes and I wanted her to know that she could tell me anything. I also needed to know the details of what happened. It hit me then that she hadn't told me who it was on the phone that caused all of this truth to come out.

I asked her who had called earlier and upset her so much? I felt like I was on an emotional roller coaster when I heard the words from her lips. "It was the police. They think they know who raped me."

Chapter 17

I needed details. I knew hearing Somara tell me about her rape would be painful. But no more painful than the actual rape was for her, and here I was asking her to relive it by telling me what happened. I listened intently to every anguish filled word.

"I had some errands to run when I got off work. I had taken care of everything except picking up my black boots from the repair shop. I started to just put it off and go home because it had gotten dark. But I figured it wouldn't take long since the shop wasn't too far from the house and it was in a small strip mall. Then I could just relax all weekend. I should have just gone home. I wish I had."

"I picked up my boots and stopped in a few of the other stores. When I got out to the car my arms were full and I didn't have my keys in my hand. I've seen those shows on T.V. that talk about being safe and being aware of your surroundings. They tell you to keep your keys in your hand and have them ready so you can get in your car quickly and lock the door right away."

"I knew all of that. I just didn't do it. I didn't even think about it. I've heard people in desperate situations so many times say, 'It happened so fast.' It did, it really did. It happened so fast, I couldn't even think."

"When I got to my car, I was digging for my keys in my purse. I gasped for air and a crushing pain was going through my stomach as my shoes were dragged right off my feet. I could feel the skin being torn off my heel by the pavement. A man had gabbed me from behind. He covered my mouth with his hand and wrapped his arm tightly around my waist as he dragged me to the grassy area near the parking lot. I just knew I was going to die."

Her voice was trembling as she told me the details. She lowered her head into her hands and just sobbed. I reached for her in an attempt to embrace her, but she pushed me away. I kissed her on the top of the head and pulled her into my body and wrapped my arms around her. I could feel her body relax into mine as she continued to cry. I held her in my arms as my own tears started to swell in my eyes. I told her that she didn't have to tell me anything else. A few minutes later she told me the rest of the story.

"I never saw his face. When he got me to the grassy area away from the buildings, he laid me face down on the ground. I felt the cold gun that he held to the back of my head as he put his knee in my back and said, 'If you scream, I will blow your brains out right here.' He blind folded me and pulled my coat down my arms. His hands were cold and rough like he might have had calluses on them. He was taller than me. I could tell, because when he grabbed me at my car, he put his hand over my mouth and pulled my body backward against him and I could feel his chin on the top of my head."

"He took his hand and slid it up my dress to pull down my panties. He must have kept my panties since the police never found them. He laid his body down on top of me. He smelled clean and I could even smell the cologne he had on. The minute he pierced my body a piece of me died that I will never get back."

"When he was finished, he whispered in my ear, 'I've always wanted you.' A security guard called the police when he found my car in the parking lot and my purse and packages were still on the ground."

I asked her if his voice sounded familiar. She said she wasn't sure but his saying that he always wanted her frightened her even more. It made her think he might attack her again since he must have known her.

I told Somara how sorry I was that she had to endure such a horrible thing. She had clearly suffered so much more than I had, even being in prison. I felt responsible since I wasn't around to protect her. If I had been home, she probably wouldn't have been out alone that night. I would have taken her to run her errands. I couldn't shake off my guilt.

We got another call from the police. Based on DNA, the police believed they had the man in custody that had raped Somara. She was glad that someone had finally been arrested. Sadly, the arrest had brought it all back to the forefront of her mind again. The police said the man had been arrested in relationship to a different case. He became a suspect in Somara's rape after his DNA was run through the police's database.

Chapter 18

Business was good and it felt good to be back on the right side of the law. I had a new client whom I had met with a few times. She had taken over a restaurant that she was awarded in the divorce settlement with her ex-husband. He handled the business and finance end of the restaurant much to their disadvantage. So wisely, she sought someone to help her restructure things and get the business in a good place financially. She had faithful clientele who frequented the restaurant on a regular basis. Her ex-husband had not handled the money end of the business well, which led her to me.

Ava Jones was a short petite woman who fit the criteria of the type of woman I found very attractive. It was easy to tell just by looking at her fine firm frame that she had never had any children. Over several weeks, we spent quite a bit of time together. We set up a different accounting and payroll system, as well as created a marketing campaign for the catering aspect of the business, which she wanted to launch in early spring.

Ava invited me to dinner at her restaurant as her way to say, "thanks" for my help, as if her hefty check didn't say, "thanks" enough. I know I should have taken Somara with me but I didn't. To my surprise, dinner was served in a private dining room. The lighting and the mood in the room were very intimate. Ava looked gorgeous in a form fitting black evening dress with a low cut back. I should say, "An almost sinfully low cut back."

I watched her walk across the room toward me. Her sexy walk and curveous hips made it hard for me not to think about how attracted I was to her. She leaned in to kiss me on the cheek and said, "Thank you for coming." I could smell her seductive perfume when she leaned in toward me. Her hair was long, almost to the middle of her back. I hadn't seen a lot of Black women up close with hair that long that wasn't a weave job. She noticed me starring at her hair. She laughed and said, "It's all mine. I mean it all grew from my scalp." I laughed, apologized for starring, and told her how beautiful it was.

Dinner was delicious. I had never eaten baked salmon teriyaki. During our after dinner conversation, I learned that she was beautiful on the outside and lonely on the inside. She had been married to her husband for seven years. The restaurant had been her idea. Her husband didn't want children. Ava had only wanted to be a mother and wife to the man she thought she would spend the rest of her life with. She said he told her to find a hobby, because he would never give her a child.

The evening was getting late. I thanked Ava for a wonderful dinner. When I stood to leave, she stepped close to me and straightened my tie. Then she put her soft, luscious, sweet lips on mine. She slowly slid her tongue into my mouth and I couldn't ignore my attraction to her any longer. Her kissing me became me kissing her.

She asked me not to leave and to please just sit and talk to her for a few minutes longer. Her eyes looked so sad. I sat down and we continued to talk. We talked over a whole bottle of White Zinfandel. She grew up in the south and learned to cook from both her mother and grandmother. She had an excellent chef but she baked all the homemade southern dishes herself, or at the very least, supervised each one. She also did a personal taste test of each dish before it was added to the menu. Between the chef, Ava, her mother, and grandmother's recipes, Ava was definitely sitting on a gold mine.

I enjoyed listening to the sound of her voice. Before I realized it two hours had passed. I knew I had to get out of there and home to Somara and David. Before I left, I asked Ava to meet me for lunch the following day.

On the drive home, I felt guilty about the time I had spent with Ava, yet still curious about what might be next. I got home late and I hadn't called Somara. She was sure to be worried about me and upset that I hadn't called to say, I would be late. I was surprised and glad to find that she was asleep.

I took a shower and got ready for bed. When I walked into our bedroom, Somara was awake. She let me know that she was a little upset with me for being so late. We talked about it briefly. Then I smoothed things over with a kiss, and a promise to call the next time I would be late. She told me she had kept my dinner in the oven and she would warm it up for me. I told her that I wasn't hungry. That wasn't a lie. I just didn't tell her why I wasn't hungry. I had already eaten dinner with another woman. We talked and cuddled. That was routine for us every night before bed. We both looked forward to that part of the evening together. It felt good as always. I asked her if she had heard from the police yet. She said no. I could hear the hurt in her voice. I held Somara tightly and told her how much I loved her.

The next morning when the alarm went off, I laid in bed holding Somara in my arms. I wasn't ready to release her from my embrace. I kissed her gently on her lips. She slept so peacefully in my arms. I knew she had to still be tired. She hadn't slept well since the phone call from the police telling her about a possible suspect being in custody. Several times since I had been home, she woke up in the middle of the night from a bad dream screaming. She wouldn't tell me what the dreams were about. But I was pretty sure the dreams had to do with the rape.

When I got to work, the morning went by quickly. I watched the clock since I was looking forward to having lunch with Ava. I didn't usually go out of the office for lunch, but I did want to see Ava's pretty smile. We met at her restaurant and had a quiet lunch in her office. We did more talking than eating lunch. I enjoyed her company. When I was with her I thought about Somara. When I was with Somara, I found myself thinking about Ava. I was in love with Somara but I was intrigued with Ava.

I continued to see her and that began to get complicated because I had started to have feelings for her. However, I hadn't been unfaithful to Somara. At least not what most men would call unfaithful. I hadn't been intimate with Ava. Most of the time we were together was spent talking and eating. I had become a regular at her restaurant. I stopped by one evening for some of her delicious homemade sweet potato pie. Instead of going to my home, like I usually did after stopping by her restaurant, I went home with her. It was definitely something I shouldn't have done.

Ava put on some soft music and poured us both a glass of wine. She kicked her shoes off and sat down next to me on her plush black leather sofa. We laughed and talked for almost an hour.

Ava stretched her warm firm legs across my lap. I slowly massaged her legs and feet. She moaned softly and told me how good it felt. Then she leaned her head backwards over the arm of the sofa. Ava looked so sexy as she poured wine down her chest and licked her lips. I watched it roll down between her breasts. I leaned over her and placed my warm wet tongue between her moist succulent breasts. The wine was sweet but the delicious taste of her skin was much sweeter.

I fondled the plump sides of her breast with my tongue. Then I gently moved from one plump side to the other nibbling on the skin in my mouth. She took quick gasping breaths with each touch of my tongue. I could feel her chest rise up and down. The slow passionate moans that she released encouraged me to over take her aroused nipples with my mouth. She gasped hard and I felt her body quiver beneath me.

I pressed my body hard against hers and took her tongue into my mouth just as she was running the tip of it over her lips. She willingly gave it to me and I sucked it as hard as I had sucked her nipples. I slowly moved my hand up the side of her thigh and under her dress. To my surprise, she wasn't wearing any panties.

I planned to just sample her wet hot insides with my finger. But once I felt the warm juicy center of her body with my finger that just wasn't enough. She wanted me as much as I wanted her. She kissed me passionately as she unzipped my pants. I was already about to explode. I slid inside of her slowly. She arched her back to meet me and feel all that I had to give her.

I made love to her like I hadn't been with a woman in a long time. With every down stroke, I wanted to go deeper and I wanted more of her. She whispered in my ear, "It's so good! Don't stop." I didn't want to disappoint her. But I needed to stop because I was about to reach my peak and I hadn't worn a condom. She squirmed beneath me like she was truly enjoying every motion we made together. I felt myself at the point of no return and she held me close to her like she knew I was about to climax and she came right along with me. I wanted to stay there with her and enjoy the feel of her soft skin next to mine. I knew that wasn't possible. Somara was at home waiting for me. I drove home with the mixed emotions of both pleasure and guilt.

It was Saturday morning and I stood in the shower trying to wash away the guilt I felt about being unfaithful to Somara. I stayed in the bathroom longer than usual. I felt like when Somara looked into my eyes, she would be able to see my infidelity. She was asleep when I got home from my evening with Ava. I was glad because I knew she would have had questions.

When Somara came downstairs, I was already drinking my first cup of coffee. She was her warm loving self as she greeted me with a kiss and told me that she loved me. She did however ask me what was going on at work that had me coming home late on a regular basis.

I knew that conversation was coming sooner or later. I told her not to worry about it. Things were under control and I wouldn't be coming home late anymore. I really loved Somara. She had been nothing but good to me and I was sure she had been faithful. I was the one who tripped so hard wondering whether she could be faithful to me and I ended up being the cheat. Not to mention a liar as well.

It was a weak moment that I should have been able to resist. I know I'm not the only brother that had an opportunity to be with a gorgeous woman other than his own and didn't turn it down. I think more often then not, a woman in the same situation might find it easier to say no, and be faithful to her man.

Now I'm not saying every woman, but I'm pretty sure most women would say, "Men just need to learn how to be faithful, and accept that they don't have to have every piece of tail they see."

I can hear Somara saying, "Don't gamble with what you're not willing to lose." She told me that shortly after we started dating. That was exactly what I had done and no way did I want to lose Somara.

Chapter 19

It had been almost a month since I'd seen Ava. She called me several times but I kept the conversations short. I knew I needed to break it off. I just didn't want her to feel like I had sexed her and then just tossed her to the side. I really did like Ava, but I loved Somara. I called Ava and asked her if I could stop by her house. Based on the enthusiasm I heard in her voice, she was glad to hear from me.

Somara was expecting me home in time for dinner, so I needed to make my visit with Ava brief. Sitting in her driveway, I tried to collect my thoughts. This fine, single, successful woman wanted me. Her husband had already dogged her. There I was about to tell her that we couldn't see each other again. I didn't feel good about being another man who had hurt her. I also didn't want to hurt Somara and I definitely meant for us to stay together.

Ava opened her front door. She was standing there looking all good and wearing the hell out of those low rider jeans. Looking at her, I was determined not to be sucked in by all of her fineness.

She smiled and ran her hand through her hair as she asked me, "So, you'd rather sit in my driveway than come into my house?" I took a deep breath and got out of my car. I walked up to the door. She stood there for a second and just looked at me, before she hugged me, and then moved aside to let me walk through the door.

I told her I was sorry that we hadn't talked much. I had been really busy at the office. The sarcasm in her response was clear, "Yeah, I guess you have been. You cancelled our last two appointments."

I didn't look forward to what I had to tell her. Prolonging it wasn't going to make it any easier. So I jumped right in with what I had to say. I tried to smile and sound upbeat while I told her that her restaurant was doing much better. The accountant that I referred her to would do an excellent job taking care of the finances which all meant that she didn't need my services any longer.

The happy look on her face quickly changed to a stern gaze. She shook her head and said, "So what are you trying to say Malcolm? You're dropping me as a client? What the hell is that?"

I tried to choose my words carefully as I spoke. "I'm sorry, Ava, this business relationship isn't going to work out and I definitely can't see you personally anymore. You're a beautiful woman with a lot to offer any man. But I'm already involved with someone and you know that. I'm not blaming you. It's my fault. I never should have let us go down this pathway in the first place." I heard myself say those words to her knowing all along not one word that had come out of my mouth would make the break up any easier for her. I wanted to tell her how bad I felt about things. I was only able to get out, "Ava I ..." She quickly cut me off.

The anger in her voice was obvious as she gave me a piece of her mind. I remember what she said to me clearly. "Oh, no, don't Ava me. You knew exactly what you were doing. Having dinner, lunch, and hanging out with me was one thing. Being intimate with me was entirely another. We took it to a different level. Right after that, all of our conversations were two minutes or less. Now you want to just break it off. Well guess what Malcolm, you don't get to walk away that easy. I'm pregnant!"

"Pregnant, you're pregnant!" Those were the only words I could get out of my mouth. I must have said it at least two more times.

She walked away from me and stood by the window. I wondered what she was thinking and why she wasn't saying anything. She broke her silence as she turned toward me. "You heard me. Yes, I'm pregnant. I've wanted a child for a long time. This wasn't planned, but there's no way I'm going to consider not having it. So don't even go there."

I told her I would never ask her to have an abortion. But I had to ask if the child was mine. She told me there was no way for the baby to be another man's since she hadn't been with anyone else but me.

I stood there in shock looking at her, wishing I could kick myself for creating such a mess. A child by a woman I wasn't in love with. By a woman that wasn't Somara. I went home and had dinner with David and Somara. I sat across the table and looked at my family, the woman that I loved, and the little boy that had come to feel like my own. I thought about how a mistake, a moment of bad judgment, could make a six-foot tall man feel so small.

Sleep didn't come easy for me that night. Somara lay in my arms unaware of my betrayal. If she had known that another woman was about to have my baby, something she hadn't been able to do, she would have been crushed.

As much as I regretted having slept with Ava, I couldn't ignore the small voice inside of me that kept saying, "I'm going to be a father. A real father since this child will be biologically mine." I was glad Somara was asleep. She would have known something was on my mind and she would have wanted to talk about it. There was no way, I could tell Somara that I had cheated on her, and definitely not that I was about to have a baby with another woman.

The next morning, the phone call we were waiting for finally came. The police wanted Somara to come down to talk about the possible suspect they had in her rape case. Somara was chewing on the end of her ink pen and rubbing her fingertips across her eyebrow like she always did when she was nervous. I kissed her gently and told her we would go down together.

We got downtown and spent thirty minutes waiting to talk to Sergeant James. He gave us some details about the suspect that was in custody and why he was thought to be the man that raped Somara. What I really wanted to know, he hadn't told us yet. I wanted to know the suspect's name. Sergeant James told us the minimum sentence if he was found guilty could be as little as five years. I felt Somara squeeze my hand several times as he went over the info with us. The look on her face when she heard him say five years concerned me.

We both looked at each and at almost the same time we both said, "That's it, five years?" The sergeant said that would be where the sentencing would start. But he hadn't seen first time rapist of adult women be sentenced to much more time than that, unless they had brutally beaten or killed their victim as well.

We were told the trial would start in a couple of months. The next words that fell out of the sergeant's mouth shook me. Money, Gavin Andrews, was the man the police had in custody for the rape of Somara over four years ago. He was the same man that had testified against me and helped to send me to prison with a twenty-year sentence. He continued to be a leech that was sucking the life out of me. Somara looked away at the wall for a moment. Just as I put my hand on her shoulder, she turned to me and said, "He told me that he always wanted me."

The tears that rolled down her face made my heart ache. I was the guilty party. I was the reason that Money even knew who

Somara was. It was then that I realized that he had planned to rape her. I didn't know it for sure, but I felt it in my gut. I didn't believe he just saw her in a parking lot and decided she was the one. The sergeant grabbed both of our attention with a reality both Somara and I hadn't thought about. There would need to be a DNA test to confirm that Money was David's father. That, of course, would be critical information in the State's case against him.

The next few weeks were filled with a myriad of emotions. The man that raped Somara was about to stand trial. Somara was glad that he was in custody but she said she wasn't looking forward to publicly reliving the rape. I was definitely glad he was behind bars. Though that didn't ease my guilt about him even knowing Somara. He only knew her because of me and that continued to nag away at my insides. Not to mention the unspoken guilt I felt about the child that Ava was pregnant with. My child!

My contact with Ava didn't end. Although that was my plan, the evening I went to her house to break things off. I had to see her and make sure she was okay. I couldn't expect her to go through nine months of being pregnant and I not be there. The real truth of it was, I wanted to be there for her. This was my first child. Something I had wanted for some time. I meant what I said when I told Ava I would be by her side until she had the baby. At the same time, I needed her to be clear that there was no possibility of a relationship for us. I didn't love her, nor was I in love with her.

That started out being the truth. I didn't expect that as the weeks passed and I could see the change in Ava's body, reluctantly my heart began to change also. I watched her belly grow with my child. She was radiant, and every day more and more full of the life that was growing inside of her. I tried not to, but my feelings for her grew.

There were two women in my life that I had feelings for. I was trying to take care of both of them. I hadn't necessarily done a good job on either count. I was totally responsible for what happened to Somara and the hell that she was still living. If I hadn't been irresponsible with Ava, she wouldn't have gotten pregnant, at least not by me.

The other person that I cared about and willingly accepted responsibility for was David. Knowing that Money was his father tore away at me every day. I tried not to let that fact change the way I felt about him. Unfortunately, the reality of Ava having my baby definitely didn't make it any easier. I wanted to still love David. I wanted him to still be my little buddy that didn't see any wrong that his daddy did. Until I knew that Money was his father, I could get past the fact that he was conceived because Somara had been raped. But knowing Money was the one who committed the rape made that close to impossible.

I started spending less one on one time with David. I really struggled with how much I cared for David and how much disdain I had in my heart for his father. I felt bad about feeling that way. Some how, once I knew Money was the man that had fathered him, I could see in his face what I hadn't seen before, and that was, how much he looked just like Money.

Somara asked me why I hadn't been spending as much time with David as usual. I told her I had just been busy with work and I was pretty tired when I got home at night. She looked at me like she was reading my mind and asked if there was something going on that I hadn't shared with her. Of course, I lied and told her everything was fine. I didn't like lying to Somara. It had become something that I had to do on a regular basis. Believe me, if you lie long enough, the lies will catch up with you. But before that happens, your lies start sounding like the truth, even to you.

It had gotten harder to check in with Ava on a regular basis and keep my home life in tact and Somara not asking where I had been or where I was going. Ava had just gotten past her first trimester. She wanted me to go with her to her next doctor's appointment. Each time she had asked before, I gave her a reason why I couldn't. But it wasn't fair to her that I didn't go. I wanted to be there when she had her first ultrasound. The thought of seeing what my child looked like growing inside of her excited me. I really did want to fully share the pregnancy with Ava.

Chapter 20

My lies were catching up with me. I was about to walk into a war zone and didn't know it. When I got home the house was unusually quiet. I started up the stairs and called out to Somara. When I reached the top of the stairs, she was standing there but she didn't say anything. Her lips were clinched shut and her cheeks were quivering. I knew she was mad. I asked her if she was all right. She quickly said, "No, not at all, and we need to talk." I followed her into our bedroom. What came next, I definitely didn't expect.

Her cheeks were still quivering when she said, "I found this receipt in the pocket of your suit jacket." She held the receipt in my face with both hands about an inch away from my nose. Her hands were shaking and so was her voice as she went straight off on me.

I don't think she took a breath at all while she lashed out at me saying, "Don't try to tell me that this was a gift for somebody because it's not just one or two things. This receipt is for a baby crib, an infant car seat, a baby monitor and a bunch of other baby stuff. Pretty much everything needed to set up a nursery. What's going on Malcolm? I'm not pregnant. So who is?"

I tried to answer her by starting with, "Baby it's not what you think." Before I could get the next words out of my mouth, she stepped closer to me and said, "It's not what I think. What do I think Malcolm? What do I think?" She was furious and rightfully so. I didn't know what to say in order not to upset her more. For sure, a complete lie like, "I don't know anything about it," wasn't going to suffice. I told Somara, I was just trying to help out a friend and there was nothing going on between us.

She looked me straight in my eyes with her response, "A female friend that I don't know about. A female friend that you are such good friends with that you go out and shop with her to furnish a nursery. You did go shopping with her, right? I mean you're the one with the receipt in your pocket. I'm sure she wanted some input on what the nursery would look like or needed, right?"

I should have thought about my next response. Because my reply, "She's been through a lot and I was just trying to help her," only angered Somara more. Not to mention the fact that it was very insensitive of me considering all that Somara had been through herself.

Unfortunately, I didn't think about that until I saw the tears in Somara's eyes as she said to me, "She's been through a lot. Are you serious? You went to prison and the man that helped send you there raped me. I went through nine months of pregnancy and had a baby by myself. You were not here for me in any of that. So don't tell me she's been through a lot."

I tried to apologize for saying that Ava had been through a lot. Those words had to be hurtful to Somara. She cut me off before I could get the words out. "You know what Malcolm. I don't want to hear any of those slick lines you used to run game with. I'm not stupid! I want to meet this friend and I want to hear you tell her that you and she can't be friends any longer. And I expect for this to happen immediately Malcolm. Immediately!"

After the tongue lashing, Somara told me how hurt and disappointed she was that I hadn't been honest with her about my so-called friendship with Ava. She and I had agreed early on in our relationship that we would not have close friendships with persons of the opposite sex. That was fine with me, because I didn't want her hanging out, leaning on, or talking on a regular basis to any man but me. When she was a little calmer, she asked me what was the woman's name. I didn't lie. I told her, "Ava." But I had to figure out how I was going to get out of having a face to face with Ava and Somara in the same room.

I regretted hurting Somara by having told her even a little bit about Ava. She, for sure, wasn't going to let me slip out of confessing something once she found the receipt. The timing was definitely bad since the rape trial was about to begin. Somara had enough on her mind without having to be concerned about me and another woman.

Over the next couple of days things didn't get any better. Somara had cooled off a little bit, but she was still very angry and hurt. Her interactions with me were not loving. I wasn't use to that. Although, I guess, I deserved it. I called Ava and told her about the conversation that Somara and I had. I told her once we left her O.B. appointment; we needed to talk about Somara's demand to meet her.

I guess that was my week for surprises. When we pulled up at Ava's doctor's office, I sat in the car looking at the Dr.'s name on the building. Dr. William Chase, the same O.B. Somara used when she was pregnant. I felt two feet tall and was reluctant to go inside. It was too late to back out. It would have been wrong of me to try anyway.

Exactly what I expected happened. Dr. Chase looked at me like he remembered me and realized the woman I was with was not the same woman I was with the last time that I saw him in his office. He examined Ava and told us that everything looked good with the exception of her blood pressure being a little too high. He said he would need to monitor that closely. So for the next couple of months she would need to see him twice instead of the normal once a month visit.

Then we got to look at the baby for the first time. I was surprised that I could so easily see the tiny body growing inside of Ava. As the doctor ran the transducer back and forth over her stomach, I couldn't believe that I was about to see my baby. She took my hand and smiled at me and said, "I'm happy that you're here with me." She quickly wiped away the tear that ran down the side of her face. We looked at our baby together and my heart was full. I felt really close to her at that moment. My feelings for her were growing into something I wasn't ready for and couldn't control.

When we got back to her house, the mood changed quickly because I needed to talk about Somara. It didn't seem right to ask Ava to tell Somara that she and I were just friends. The fact that I was starting to have feelings for Ava just complicated things more.

Ava was upset that I still didn't want to tell Somara about the baby. She said she didn't want to cause a problem for Somara and me, but she needed to be honest with me. She looked so sexy sitting there in her black stretch knit maternity dress that was clinging to her perky breast and the little bulge in her belly.

I could tell she was trying not to cry as her eyes watered up, her voice kept going up and down. She cleared her throat and then said to me, "Neither of us thought that we would end up having a baby together. I desired you so much that night. I just let myself go with you. I'm not even sure how we ended up being intimate. I know it wasn't what either of us planned when the evening began. Now here we are about to have a baby. Malcolm, I'm pretty sure that you don't want to hear this, but I'm falling in love with you. I can't help it, and I can't continue to act like I don't have feelings for you."

I wanted to tell Ava that I was starting to have serious feelings for her too. But that would have only made things worse. I tried to say gently that, "Right now, I have to make sure that Somara doesn't know that you're carrying my baby. That's all I can deal with, at least for now."

The look on her face said, "I can't believe what you just said to me." Then she rubbed her belly as she told me, "Your girlfriend will probably be able to tell that I have feelings for you, and I doubt very seriously that she is completely convinced that this baby is not yours. You know we women have a sixth sense."

I knew she was right. Somara was a smart woman. I didn't want to admit it to myself, but I figured the main reason Somara wanted to meet Ava was to look into her eyes. She also wanted to see how Ava would act around me, and to be sure that whoever the other woman was, she was aware that Somara knew about her. What scared me the most was knowing that the minute Somara knew for sure what was going on between Ava and me, she would walk out of my life.

We continued to talk about how to make the crazy meeting between the three of us happen without it being a disaster. Ava promised me that she wouldn't do or say anything that would give away our relationship to Somara. It was asking a lot. But once again in my life, I had no other options.

I called Somara and told her I was going to pick her up from work and we would meet Ava at a restaurant close to Somara's job. She was quiet for a few seconds and then told me she would call Donna and have her pick David up from school. David liked it when Donna would baby sit for him because she had a little boy close to his age. Before she hung up, Somara asked me a question I guess I should have expected from her at some point.

She said, "Malcolm, don't lie to me. Just tell me the truth. Do you love her?" Somara's voice sounded like it was filled with pain and the anxiety of what my answer would be. Quickly I told her, "No! I don't love her. You are the woman that I love." I heard her take a deep breath and exhale. I knew she was hurting. I also knew the word "No" was what she needed to hear me say.

The drive to meet Ava was uncomfortably quiet. Neither of us was looking forward to the back and forth question and answer session we were headed off to. When we pulled up, I didn't see Ava's car. I was glad that we had gotten there first. I opened the door and took Somara's hand to help her out of the car. When she was standing face to face with me, I thought back to the first time I saw her and how quickly I had fallen in love with her. I couldn't believe things had changed so much that I was about to introduce Somara to the woman that was carrying my baby.

We were on our second cup of coffee when I noticed Ava. She struggled to pull the door open against the heavy winds. Her long hair blew behind her. The way she moved the scattered strans from over her eyes with her fingers was sexy to me. The long black wool sweater dress she wore didn't easily reveal any hint of her being pregnant.

She saw me and walked straight back to the table where Somara and I were sitting. I was definitely a brother in the hot seat. I tried to stay calm as I introduced Somara and Ava to each other. Neither of them smiled at the other but both cordially said, "Hello." Right away Somara took the lead. The conversation between them was swift and to the point.

"Let's make this brief and to the point. Ava, I'm sure you know why we're here. How do you know Malcolm and why is he buying things for your baby?"

"I was a client of Malcolm's. He helped me get my business restructured and setup with a good accountant. In the course of casual conversation, he mentioned you, and how much he loved you. I talked about my ex-husband and my recent divorce. We became friends. Yes, he bought some things for my baby, but it was innocent. He was just trying to help me out."

"So what does that mean? You couldn't afford to furnish your own nursery?" Somara's tone was unfriendly and firm to say the least.

Ava's response wasn't as defensive as I halfway expected it to be. She simply replied, "My business is just now starting to turn around financially. It was just a nice thing for him to do."

"Okay, how about you try getting your ex-husband to do the next nice thing you need done. It is his baby, right?" Somara's responses and questions so quickly followed the last word out of Ava's mouth it was unnerving.

Ava remained calm and politely answered, "Yes, the baby is my ex-husbands."

Somara looked over at me and then at Ava and said, "So you're telling me the baby is not Malcolm's?"

I had a knot in my stomach after hearing Somara's question. Because I was nervous about Ava's answer. Somehow, Ava sounded convincing when she responded, "No! It's not."

Somara stared at Ava for an uncomfortable few seconds. Then looking me straight in the eyes like she wanted to see into my heart and pierce my soul for a truthful answer, she asked me, "Is the baby yours?"

"No, Ava's baby is not mine. We're just friends. I understand that our friendship makes you uncomfortable. I won't see her again." I didn't look away from her gaze as I lied to her. I wanted to. I really didn't want to sit in her face and lie through my teeth. But there it was, a resounding "no" and an irreversibly hurtful lie.

"Are you in love with Malcolm?" I could see that Somara was listening with her eyes, ears, and her heart for Ava's response.

I know the words that came out of Ava's mouth were hard for her. She still did what I needed her to do by denying her feelings for me in her answer to Somara. "I would be lying if I said, I don't care for Malcolm. He's my friend, and I wish nothing but good things for him. But I'm not in love with Malcolm." Hearing her say, "I'm not in love with Malcolm." stung a little. Though I knew it wasn't true.

Somara pushed the coffee cup in front of her into the middle of the table. She looked at me with a cold piercing stare. Then she turned and hurled the same stare at Ava while she said, "That's good! Then you won't have a problem discontinuing your business relationship and your friendship with him and I trust that we won't need to have this conversation again."

Somara stood and waited for me to stand also. Ava started to say something but Somara ignored her. She took my hand and we walked out together. I drove Somara back to her job to pick up her car. On the ride there, she never said a word. She quickly got out of my car and slammed the door. As I followed Somara home, Ava called me on my cell phone. She was brief and to the point just as Somara had been with her.

"If Somara should ever ask me again, if I love you, I won't lie. I'm carrying your child Malcolm and I do want to be with you. Don't worry; I'm not going to make this thing any uglier than it already is. Maybe I just need to do this by myself, and you just need to focus on Somara. That is the woman you love, right?" Before I could even respond, the dial tone was buzzing in my ear.

Chapter 21

More time than we expected had past. Finally, the rape trial was about to start and Somara hadn't been sleeping well at all. She was having nightmares about the rape and being face to face with the man that had raped her. I was having trouble sleeping also. My concern for both the women in my life wouldn't let me sleep peacefully at all.

I planned to be right by Somara's side every step of the way. I hadn't been there before when this insanity all started because of my being in prison. At all cost, I would support her and do all I could to make her feel safe; something I couldn't do for her before.

Ava played a roll in my sleepless nights as well. She was hurt that I had lied to Somara about the baby. She understood that for me, the lie was necessary. But that didn't make it hurt her any less. She stopped taking my calls and wouldn't answer her door when I stopped by her house. I needed to find a way to get Ava to talk to me. She was definitely on my mind every day.

The trial finally started and it was ugly. Somara was a strong woman. Her strength was tested more than she expected as she sat in the courtroom each day. She wore her anguish in the circles under her eyes, the way she looked behind her constantly when she was out in public, and the nightmares that claimed her peaceful rest almost nightly.

Listening to the opening statements took me back to my own trial. I pushed those memories aside and thought about the baby that had come out of this tragedy. A few weeks before the trial started, we had gotten the results of the DNA test on David. It confirmed what we already knew to be true. Money was his father, which meant Money was the man that had raped Somara.

I watched Somara ride an emotional roller coaster that was tormenting her and there was nothing that I could do about it. When she took the stand to testify about the night she was raped, it felt like my skin was crawling with every ugly detail she shared. Tears pooled in her eyes that she couldn't hold back. I could see her cheek quivering; the tears roll down her face and stop at the corner of her mouth before falling onto her chest.

I heard her say the same words she said to me about being dragged across the parking lot by her heels and fearing that she would be killed. Listening to her tell the jury about it made the anger inside me build again. Just like it did the first time I heard her say the words. I clinched my fist so hard, I could feel my pulse throbbing in the palm of my hand.

Sitting in the courtroom moving my attention from Somara to Money as I watched him stare at her with a slight smile on his face, required a great deal of self-restraint on my part. I thought about the hell he had put Somara through and the almost satisfied look he had on his face. When the guard escorted him in and seated him at the table with his lawyer, he looked over at Somara and winked. I wanted to put my hands around his throat.

That demon had made me doubt what I felt for David. I was bitter and withdrawn from him for a while because knowing that Money was his father made me question whether I could love him. But I already loved him. I didn't take my eyes off Money as I thought about the day, in my front yard, that my feelings for David became crystal clear to me.

Watching David gasping for air, the rise and fall of his chest as he struggled to breath, gave me the answer I needed. I grabbed him up in my arms and ran into the house yelling

Somara's name. She hurried down the stairs toward the sound of my voice. She saw me holding him in my arms and grabbed the epinephrine injection that she kept in the kitchen drawer.

The seconds that I watched him struggle to breath cleared up the doubt in my mind about what I felt for David. It was the first time I had seen him have an allergic reaction like that. Some type of insect that he was allergic to must have bitten him while we were outside. The thought of him dying in my arms and the plea that I saw in his eyes that seemed to be saying, "Daddy help me," made it clear in my heart that no matter what, David was my son and I loved him.

I could hardly keep sitting in my seat. Money deserved to have that smug look on his faced wiped off. Somara finished her testimony. She stepped down from the witness stand and fixed her eyes on Money. She held her eye-to-eye assault on him until she reached her seat next to her attorney. She faced him head on as if to let him know he wasn't in control and she wasn't afraid of him. I was proud of her and glad to see her facing that ugly shadow of fear that had haunted her.

The prosecution rested its case. It was a Friday. The weekend would give Somara the time I thought she needed to regroup. Money's defense attorney would be making opening statements the following Monday and the next chapter in the horror story would begin.

On the drive home, Somara held my hand the whole way. She gazed out of the window as if she was sightseeing in a new city. I softly called her name. She didn't respond. I waited a few seconds, squeezed her hand and told her that I loved her. She turned to me with a slight smile on her face and leaned over and kissed me on my cheek. In a soft voice, she started to talk.

"You know what, I was afraid to be in court today. I didn't think I could look him in the face and not cry. I felt like if I looked at him eye to eye he would some how have my soul too. He already took my dignity and my self-respect. He took a piece of me, a piece of who I am as a woman that I can't take back. I couldn't let him have my soul."

"That was why I had to look at him. I needed him to see that I was in control, not him. That he couldn't take the heart of me because that really defines who I am as a person. I couldn't have done that without you sitting in the courtroom. When I was testifying, the words were coming out of my mouth. But my thoughts weren't in that courtroom. I thought about when we first met, when I fell in love with you, and all that we've been through together, and the fact that I want us to be whole again. When I walked across the room staring at that monster, I held on to those thoughts. Thank you Malcolm for being there with me. I love you so much!"

I still think about those words that she said to me that day. The sentiment in her voice when she said, "I love you so much!" made me feel so good. Often, late at night, I try to hear her voice saying, I love you, with that same sentiment.

We made love that night. It was passionate and long, like she couldn't get enough of me. Our love making finally felt like it had before I went away to prison. Ever since I had been home, it seemed like something was missing in her, almost like she wasn't whole and definitely the way she made love to me wasn't whole. I guess she couldn't be whole. Not until that day in the courtroom when she took something back from Money that was never his.

The weekend seemed long to me. I'm sure that was because I was determined to try and tear down the communication barrier put up by Ava. I went to her restaurant to try and talk to her. I knew she wouldn't want to make a scene there. She agreed to talk with me briefly in her office.

Sitting in Ava's office, waiting for her, I was drawn to a specific painting that hung on the wall. A silhouette of a pregnant woman from the neck down wrapped in a red satin sheet held my attention. Since the woman in the painting didn't have a face, I gave her one.

I could see Somara's happy face beaming with the joy of taking a pregnancy to full term. I drifted back to when she told me she was pregnant. Sitting there, I could almost feel the warmth from her body when I wrapped my arms around her pregnant belly at night when we slept. She wanted so much to have a baby and I wanted that for us.

As I pictured Ava's face in the painting, the visit to the doctor's office for her first ultrasound came to mind. I wanted to be a part of my child's life, not just a pass by daddy. Looking at my child growing inside of her made me want to be the kind of father that's on the job on a regular basis. Not just around occasionally to buy milk and pampers.

It wasn't until Ava asked me why was I staring at the painting that I realized she had walked into the office. I thanked her for seeing me and I asked her if we could please talk.

She was defensive in her response, "Talk about what Malcolm? You talked enough for me when you told Somara, 'No, Ava's baby is not mine.' What else is there for us to talk about?"

My initial response to her was sterner than I meant for it to be. "You know why I had to say that. I understand that it hurt you. But let's be real with each other. You knew about Somara when we started this. I'm not trying to be cold, but Somara's not going anywhere. I need and want to be a part of this baby's life and I want to be there for you when you need me. Not just when the baby is born but while you're pregnant too. Don't take that away from me." I didn't know how to be gentle and be real with her at the same time.

As I think back to that conversation, it still saddens me now. She cried when she said, "It's really hard for me to be around you and know that you're in love with another woman. You sleep with her every night and that's the woman that you have feelings for."

I tried to be honest with Ava by telling her that I had sincere feelings for her, but the love triangle wasn't going to work. Somara was never a secret. She had known about her from the beginning and I didn't want her hurt.

Ava stepped closer to me. She ran her hands over the top of her stomach and cupped them under the bottom. Her little watermelon belly looked so sexy to me. She knew that. How a man can't be attracted to a sexy woman carrying his baby is beyond me. She took my hand and placed it on her belly. I felt my baby moving inside of her for the first time. I couldn't believe I was touching the life that was growing inside of her body. She smiled at me, and seconds later we were engrossed in a kiss that tasted so sweet.

She never stopped kissing me while she walked me backwards over to the love seat in her office. I dropped down onto the love seat as she straddled my lap. She raised her dress up to her thighs as I quickly squeezed them to feel her soft skin in my hands. Her neck smelled good and she moaned softly as I licked her neck and kissed behind her ear.

Ava raised her body up and leaned her breast into me. I slide her panties to the side and lowered her down on top of me. She gasped as I entered her body and we enjoyed each other intensely and the warmth inside of her made it hard for me to take my time. Minutes later she relaxed her body against my chest and again I could feel my child moving wildly inside of her belly. I could not resist Ava. I knew that making love to her was only complicating things further. My attempts to ignore my feelings for her were absolutely impossible when I was in her presence. I was creating a precarious situation that no one would escape unhurt.

Chapter 22

The weekend was over and, for the second time, I had been intimate with Ava. My heart continued to soften for her even though my mind was telling me to control what I felt for her, because there needed to be only one woman that I was romantically involved with.

I've heard women say, "A man can't truly care for two women. One might have his heart but the other is just a booty call." I know for myself that is definitely not true. Both of these women had a special place in my heart. However, I knew there couldn't be a happy ending all the way around, but I couldn't break it off with either of them.

I stood looking out of the window early Monday morning, feeling guilty once again about being unfaithful to Somara. She lay there still sleeping as the sun was rising and starting to light up our bedroom. For the first time, I was also feeling guilty about being with Somara and leaving Ava all alone. I had gotten myself into a situation that didn't have an easy solution.

David went off to school and Somara and I got ready for court. She put on a dark blue suit that fit her nicely and complimented her hips. I liked to watch her get dressed. Her breast, which sat up perky and attentive on their own without the use of an under wire bra, always turned me on.

She sat down on the handcrafted bed bench at the foot of our bed to put on her shoes. I remember when I surprised her by having the bench delivered about two weeks after we moved into the house. She loved it and said she had always wanted one of those. After putting on one shoe, she turned and looked at me and asked, "Have you seen Ava?" I swallowed hard while I closed the door to my walk-in closet. I hoped that she couldn't hear the lie in my voice as I answered her, "No, I haven't baby." She was still looking right into my eyes. I half expected her to call me a liar. But she didn't. She said, "I love you!"

I wondered if she knew I was still seeing Ava but just didn't want to deal with it then, or if she knew and just chose not to deal with it. I hoped that she wouldn't find out and somehow the mess I had made would work out with no one being hurt any more than they already were.

We got to court and I sat in my then usual spot right behind Somara. Sitting there, I thought about all the years that had past between the rape and the trial. If he hadn't been arrested for another crime and his DNA taken, he probably would have gotten away with what he did to Somara.

The defense began presenting its case. I guess Money thought it would be to his advantage to have a female attorney defending him in a rape trial. She gave her opening statement to the jury of five women and seven men. All of who seemed to be hanging on her every word.

She painted a totally different picture of what went down with Somara and Money the night she was raped. She told the jury that there was sex involved but the sex was consensual. She wanted the jury to believe that once I was sentenced, Somara and Money had actually rekindled an affair they started several months before I had been arrested. The affair went on until Somara became pregnant. Soon after that, Money broke it off with her. Angry about the unexpected breakup, she didn't tell him that she was pregnant.

Miss Davis, Money's defense attorney, sounded so convincing when she said, "Of course, Ms. Hughes had to come up with some type of story to tell her man. Especially since he was still serving time in the Federal Penitentiary system when she got pregnant. She knew he would be coming home and she couldn't very well tell him, 'Oh, by the way, I had a baby by the man who testified against you at your trial.' So she came up with this elaborate story about being raped." The lies were his but the smooth articulate tongue that delivered them was definitely that of a skillful attorney that knew how to deliver a speech.

The defense attorney looked at Somara with a confident smerk as she told the jury, "If there was indeed a rape, my client didn't commit that rape. He admits to having sex with Ms. Hughes the very night in question. That was also the night he broke things off with her. So who is to say that she didn't have sex willingly with someone else or perhaps someone else raped her after she had been intimate with my client."

She went on to say, "Mr. Andrews doesn't deny that his DNA matches that of Ms. Hughe's son. However, Mr. Andrews had no idea that he had fathered a child with Ms. Hughes. He is excited to know that he has a son and wants very much to be a part of his life."

The trial continued for six days. In her closing arguments Miss. Davis tried to damage Somara's credibility even more. I could see Somara fighting back the tears as she listened to the defense attorney tell the jury, "There was an unfortunate miscarriage in Ms. Hughes' past that shattered her dream of having a child. So even though another man had fathered her son, she finally had the child that she wanted so badly. She would just have to find a way to explain her infidelity that had resulted in a child. Thus this elaborate story of a rape." I didn't have to wonder how she knew about Somara's miscarriage. Her client, Money, or Gavin Andrews, as she knew him, had armed her with everything he knew about Somara and me.

She even went on to try to make Money look like he had a conscience by saying, "Mr. Andrews' DNA was obtained illegally in association with a previous conviction that did not mandate a DNA sample. That violated Mr. Andrew's 4th Amendment rights. But since he had nothing to hide in regards to being intimate with Ms. Hughes, against my advice, he instructed me to not file a motion to suppress his DNA. Does that sound like the actions of a rapist?"

The judge gave the jury their instructions and dismissed them to the jury chambers to make a decision that would forever impact Somara's life. She and I left the courtroom and took a walk downtown. We talked about how the verdict would come back. We both hoped that the jury didn't come back to quick because that might mean they had believed his lies.

After we had an early dinner, we started for home thinking that we might not get a verdict until the following day. Somara's cell phone rang, and it was her attorney. The verdict was in. I would have done a U turn right in the middle of the street but, ironically, there was a cop right behind me. Fifteen minutes later, we were back downtown and walking into the courthouse.

"All rise." Those words almost echoed in my ears when the bailiff spoke them. The judge entered the courtroom and we all stood. Money looked over at Somara and smiled slightly then nodded his head. The jury walked in and the judge asked if they were ready to deliver their verdict. During the next few seconds, before we heard the verdict, I felt nauseous.

The judge looked at the verdict before it was read aloud. The jury foreman opened the slip of paper. She looked at the judge and delivered the unanimous decision of the jury. "Not guilty!" My attention immediately moved from the jury foreman to Somara. Her body was still in the motion of dropping down into her seat next to her attorney. My nauseous feeling came back. The judge thanked the jury for their service. Money thanked the judge and shook his attorney's hand as soon as the judge said, "Mr. Andrews, you're free to go."

The noisy sound of people leaving the courtroom became audible. I reached over the short wall like barrier that separated me from Somara and her attorney. She stood and leaned over into my arms. I held her tightly and I just kept saying, "I got you baby, I got you."

I lifted Somara's head from my chest and kissed her lips gently. The salty tears that flowed from her eyes tainted her usually sweet lips. Somara's attorney spoke to her briefly and left the courtroom. We were the last to leave. We walked down the short isle toward the door, I remember Somara saying to me as she leaned her head on my shoulder, "Now what?"

Chapter 23

Three months had past and the winter winds of Chicago were in full affect. Somara was spending a lot of time inside. Almost going nowhere other than to work and home. She managed to do the grocery shopping and not much else. I tried talking to her about what she was feeling. The most that she would tell me was that she feared Money attacking her again and that he would eventually try to contact her about seeing David.

I shared her concern so I tried to assure her that I would do everything within my power to keep her and David safe. Encouraging Somara to talk to me about her feelings, and trying to get home to her and David before dark every evening didn't seem to help much. I asked her to please consider seeing a counselor of some kind. Somara said she would think about it. However, I didn't get the feeling that she was going to do much more than that.

Trying to balance my time and share my heart meant things were still complicated because I still had two women in my life. Ava was seven months pregnant and she wanted more of my time. She said she was having trouble sleeping at night. Her balance was off and that scared her. It scared me too. I had lost my first child because Somara had a bad fall. I didn't want that to happen again. To be honest, I wanted very much to be with Ava all the time. It was the last couple of months of her pregnancy and I had already missed too much of it.

My feelings were growing for Ava, even though I still didn't want to admit that to her. Actually, I was falling in love with Ava. What I felt for her was based on more than just her carrying my child. I had gotten a chance to see the gentle side of her and that she was a good woman. During and after Somara's rape trial, she tried to be patient and caring about my situation with Somara. I could see that she cared very much for me and she was concerned about what Somara was going through.

I started going to my office less and spending a lot of my days with Ava. As much as I could, I worked from her house. She hired a manager for her restaurant so she could stay off of her feet, and she would have someone to take care of it when she had the baby. I enjoyed being with her and taking care of her. She looked so cute trying to get up off the sofa and waddling around because she was soo pregnant, she couldn't stand up straight when she walked. She had to lean backwards.

Playing house with her in the daytime just made me want to be with her more and more. I'd heard brothers talk about how good the loving is when a woman is pregnant. Really pregnant! When her body is full of your baby, her belly is plump, her sweet juices are flowing, and her insides are burning hot. Now I know for myself that the loving is extra good.

Ava wanted to make love every day and I was definitely willing to meet her needs. I thought the more along women were in their pregnancy, the less they desired sex, or felt like having sex. If that's true, it sure wasn't true for Ava. Her pregnant belly didn't keep her from being sexy, hot or desirable. This woman was under my skin. It was like it was when I first fell in love with Somara. I wanted her around me all the time and I couldn't get enough of her. Ava had the same affect on me. It all seems like yesterday. Though it wasn't, the memories of it all are still so vivid.

I had made almost every doctors appointment with her and we were about to start Lamaze class. The class would teach us about birthing techniques, stages of labor, newborn care, and breast-feeding. I planned on being right there with Ava helping her to give birth to my baby. The thought of that really made me happy, also a little nervous but happy.

Along with Ava's cravings for me, she had some crazy food cravings also. I went out for a lot of chilidogs, strawberry shortcake and pickles. Occasionally, she wanted to eat Argo cornstarch for some reason. I always tried to talk her out of it. Cornstarch just didn't seem healthy for her or the baby.

Ava didn't have much family, only her mother, and one sister, Jalese. At least that's all the family she ever told me about. Her mother, Gail Jones, lived in California and her sister in Denver. She said the three of them were very close. So, I wasn't surprised when she said they both wanted to come and be with her when she had the baby. Ava did, however, surprise me when she said she didn't want them to come for the birth.

Ava wanted her family to wait and come a few weeks after she had the baby. She wanted us to be able to bond with the baby alone. At first I thought that was a little odd. Especially since this was Ava's first child and the Christmas holiday was a couple of weeks away. I figured she would want the help of her mother with a newborn. When she told me about the conversation that she and her mom had, I understood why she didn't want them to come right away.

She made that decision after having a heated argument with her mother about her dating a man that was practically married to another woman. She said her mother's very direct words continued to ring in her ears. A week later her mother wrote her a letter, which Ava let me read.

Ava,

Let me start by saying, I love you sweetie! You are my precious daughter, my little girl. I know you're a thirty-two year old grown woman. But you will always be my little girl. You are also grown enough to know that getting involved with a man who is already involved with someone else is not only disrespectful to her but also disrespectful to you. There is also no future in it for you.

If he'll cheat on her, he'll cheat on you. Men can only cheat on their woman, if women let them. Women have to demand respect from a man. If you know he's involved with someone, then let him know that you're not going to help him cheat on her. At some point in your life, you may want to get married. Wouldn't you want other women to respect the fact that your husband has a wife?

Not only is this man that you're pregnant by involved with another woman, he lives with her and they have a son. I know you said that the little boy is not biologically his and that's why he is so excited about the child that you're carrying. But, Baby you have to know that the game you're involved in can only cause sorrow and heartbreak for somebody. I'm afraid that you might be that somebody.

He can't spend the night with you because he's home sleeping with his woman. Baby, you deserve better than that. I'm very disappointed in the choice that you've made regarding this man, but I love you and I'm here for you and whatever you might need. Please don't let my honesty with you about my feelings with this situation that you're in keep you from leaning on your mother. Remember that's what we're here for and what we do best. But then, you'll soon learn that because you're about to be a mother yourself.
Loving you always, no matter what!
Your Mother

After reading the letter, I felt even worse about the threesome that I had created. Ava was very close to her mom and I regretted being part of the reason why her mom was disappointed in her.

So there I was with two families, two women, and two children that I cared about very much. I didn't know what was going to happen next. Though I had a funny feeling, it was something that I wouldn't like. I wasn't the brother that was just purposely trying to be a player and having more than one woman. At least I wasn't that brother any more.

I had grown emotionally, and as a man, because of my relationship with Somara. Ironically, it was because of her that I could genuinely care for Ava, and be excited about the chance to be a father, knowing that the child growing inside of her was mine. A seed that I had planted and wanted to see grow.

At the same time, that took nothing away from what I felt for Somara and David. I loved them too. I had even loved them first. I knew things couldn't go on the way they were. Two families, two different lives, two different women, I knew I had to change something. Or, something was going to change on its own. Either way, it wasn't going to be pretty and somebody was going to be hurt.

Chapter 24

The holidays had past and although it was tough to spend time with both women the way I wanted to, I had an enjoyable holiday season. I made sure I showered them both with love and attention. David got everything he put on his Christmas list. My little man believed in Santa Claus. That's why Somara and I made sure he was able to write his letter to Santa and mail it off to the North Pole. Of course, we had to bake cookies for Santa on Christmas Eve. I got to use my video camera to record the holiday memories.

It was a new year and Somara was starting to feel a little better. She hadn't heard anything from Money and we were both hoping that he would just walk away. He had gotten away with raping Somara and his lies had successfully kept him from serving time. I wanted Somara and David to be able to move on without any fear of Money forcing his way into David's life.

David and I were outside shoveling snow. Well, I was shoveling snow. David had his little plastic shovel and he was trying to move the heavy snow off the front steps. I had to break out the video camera again. How a man can have a son and not want to spend time with him, watch him grow up, and teach him how to be man, I'll never understand.

I was starting to teach David how to be a little gentleman. He would hold the door for his mom and seat her when we went out to dinner. I wanted him to know how to appreciate a woman. He wasn't too young to start learning that.

We were almost finished shoveling the snow when the mailman started up our sidewalk. David saw him and off he went to get our mail. He had made friends with the mailman. He loved reaching into that big bag and pulling out our mail. It was nice of the mailman to put everything he had for us in the corner of his bag and point it out for David to reach in and grab.

David ran back down the sidewalk yelling, "I got it daddy, I got it." He handed me the mail and I sifted through the envelopes. I stopped in almost a frozen state when I saw the name and address in the return corner of the envelope. I stared at the name Gavin Andrews and couldn't believe that was really what I was seeing. Money had written Somara. I refused to refer to him as Gavin. To me he was the slick, money hungry, drug deal'n, lying brother that I knew him as. Gavin Andrews was a character that he had created for his court appearances.

As I looked at his name, I thought about how Somara had just started to come out of her morose mood. It was good to see her not be so gloomy. The letter that I held in my hand changed that. I took David inside and asked Somara to give him a snack and meet me upstairs.

She came into our bedroom with a smile on her face and closed the door. I watched her walk over to the chaise where I was sitting. Somara had that look in her eye like she wanted to get busy. I wished that had been the reason why I had told her to meet me upstairs. She put her knee between my legs and leaned her body down on top of me. I kissed her gently and pulled her over on her back to lay next to me.

I handed her the letter as the mournful words came out of my mouth, "This just came in the mail for you." Somara reached for the envelope and looked at the name in the corner. She took a deep breath and was totally silent for at least a minute. Then she ripped the seal off the envelope and tossed it to the floor. She was still lying in my arms. That made it easy for me to read the letter right along with her.

Somara,

I waited until the holidays were over to contact you. I hope my son had a Merry Christmas and Santa was able to bring him everything he wanted. That probably wasn't a problem, right? I'm pretty sure that my man Malcolm made that happen.

I imagine that you've been wondering if and when you would hear from me. I meant what I said in court. I want to be a part of my son's life. Since the jury found me innocent, there's no reason why that can't happen. You might have even missed my touch and maybe you and I can start where we left off. That can definitely be arranged.

I'm going to give you a little time to get use to the idea of having to share my son with me. But don't be mistaken; I am going to see him. So, you can call me on my cell at 708-512-3566 or you can drop by the return address on the envelope. That's where I'm staying and I wanted you to know how to get in touch with me in case my son needed anything.

Gavin

Somara was too quiet and that concerned me. I wanted to wait for her to say something. Not a sound came out of her mouth. She just kept lying there. I pulled her to me as I looked into her eyes for my answer. I asked her if she was okay? Her sad words pulled at my heart, "Malcolm, you can't let this happen." The look in her face was filled with anguish. She wrapped her arms around my neck. I meant what I said to her, "I promise you, I don't know how, but Money will never spend one second with our son."

That day was long and it didn't seem like it would ever end. We ate dinner and spent the evening watching movies with David. I gave him his bath and put him to bed. When I got back to the family room, Somara was going through all the pictures she had of David. There were picture albums and loose pictures lying all over the floor.

I sat down beside her and we looked at every photo. I especially enjoyed looking at the ones of the first three years of David's life, which I had missed. We laughed and talked about all the cute little things he was doing in each picture. It felt good laughing and talking with Somara as she walked me through the first few years of his life. I had often said I was going to take the time to go through all those pictures. But once I got home from prison, I was too busy living in the moment of coming home to a family and learning how to be a dad.

Somara and I talked about Christmas and how wonderful it was sharing it with David. Seeing Christmas through his eyes reminded us of what Christmas was really all about. She wanted to talk about how I planned on making sure Money wasn't a part of David's life. But I told her not to worry about it. I would take care of it. I just wanted her to be happy and enjoy being his mother.

Chapter 25

Ava was two weeks away from her due date. I had gotten a pager for her to use to contact me if she went into labor and I wasn't with her. She was the only person with the number and she was to page me using 911 when it was time. That way I didn't have to worry about checking my cell phone all the time and missing her call. That's because anyone might have been calling me on my cell phone. I was nervous and could hardly sleep because I was afraid I might miss the page.

Ava was seeing her obstetrician every week. Her blood pressure was high and she had some swelling in her hands and feet. She was also experiencing some unexplainable abdominal pain. So the doctor had placed her on complete bed rest for the last two weeks of her pregnancy. For me that meant I needed to be with her more in order to take care of her. Over the next few days I spent as much time as possible with Ava. I even left home at night a few times to check on her quickly, and then rushed back home to David and Somara.

She was also having a hard time sleeping because the baby was very active at night. The morning I took her to the last doctor's appointment before she had the baby, Ava had only slept four hours the night before. I spent ten minutes massaging her belly trying to get the baby to move its elbow from under Ava's rib cage before we even left for the doctor's office.

The doctor's appointment went well. Ava's blood pressure was down and the baby's heart rate was good. Dr. Chase said the baby should weigh some where between six and a half to seven pounds. The baby didn't appear to be in any distress and the doctor hoped Ava would be able to deliver the baby vaginally. She had already dilated two centimeters and she really did not want to have a Cesarean Section.

We had to leave the doctor's office to go over to the hospital to have some blood work done, and tests run, to continue to rule out pre-eclampsia. Her doctor had been keeping a close watch on that since high blood pressure, swelling of the face and hands and abdominal pain were all symptoms of pre-eclampsia. We were at the hospital for about two hours and I was ready to get Ava back to her house and settled. I kept watching the clock because I needed to be getting home to Somara soon.

After we got downstairs and halfway out of the emergency room door, I saw Somara running across the parking lot toward the emergency room doors. For a few seconds, she didn't realize it was me she was running toward. I had my arm around Ava and I had just rubbed her belly for the baby to calm down and be still.

Somara was a couple of feet away from me when she stopped running and walked slowly up to Ava and me. I was facing the inevitable, the hurt that's caused when you cheat. She looked at me with an expression I can't even explain. Then she looked over at Ava and said, "You sorry slut!" She didn't stop there. Before I could say a word she slapped me so hard, the side of my face stung. Her words stung even more but they were true.

"You lie as effortlessly as I breathe. I knew in my heart that baby was yours. You looked me in my face and said the baby wasn't yours and you would not be seeing her anymore. You had the audacity to come home to me every night and sleep in the same bed with me, no doubt, after you had gotten out of the bed with her."

"I've been good to you. I took care of your brother's funeral, including cleaning out his apartment and storing the things I thought you might want, and selling the rest. You are the reason I was raped. You exposed me to a crazy and dangerous life style that I was totally unaware of. But I never left your side. Is this how you repay me?"

"I could have cheated on you many times. I was lonely and out here going through hell when you were locked up for three and a half years. But I was faithful. Did you tell Miss Thang that you went to prison on a drug charge? Probably not! But then she probably wouldn't have cared anyway. Most tramps don't when all they're looking for is a hard rod and a warm body."

Somara looked at me from head to toe as she said to Ava, "Well, you can definitely have his cheat'n behind." She wasn't too loud as to draw attention but she was definitely firm with every word that she delivered. I wanted to say something but I was totally caught off guard.

Before she walked away, Somara said, "Oh yeah, Malcolm, I just happened to run into you here at the hospital because your son fell and broke his arm on the play ground at school. But don't let that stop you from taking your baby's mama wherever it is you were both off to. Your clothes will be packed and sitting on the porch. Don't bother coming back, and by the way, I'll be keeping the house. Remember, you put it in my name. Thanks!" Her laughter rang out behind her as she walked away.

What had happened was just like a dream. Ava had to tug on my jacket and call my name for me to snap out of it. She sounded very calm when she said, "I'm sorry she had to find out like this, Baby. I know she's hurt but we've got a little one to think about." Ava didn't seem to be concerned about David. I guess she felt like she had won somehow.

I was torn emotionally because I wanted to go and see about my son. But I didn't want to upset Somara anymore than she already was. I finally moved from the doorway of the hospital and took Ava to her house. I told her to call me if she needed anything. I had to get out of there and be by myself for a little bit. Ava said she couldn't believe I was leaving because we could finally spend the night together. Ava's concern was only for herself. I couldn't even be mad at her. She had been in the background for nine months. I guess she felt like it was her turn to be front and center.

I drove around wishing I could kick myself for the mess I had made of things. I never wanted Somara to hate me. Those weren't her words, but I was pretty sure those were her feelings at the time. She was right. She had been nothing but good to me. Better than I deserved actually. I had repaid her with lies on top of lies and the ultimate betrayal, infidelity.

Chapter 26

I pulled up in the driveway of our house in Olympia Fields. Somara was true to her word. My leather personalized luggage was packed and sitting on the porch. That wasn't everything, but I was sure she was working on packing the rest of my things. I sat there in the driveway with the car running for almost an hour. I wanted to go inside although I wasn't looking forward to seeing the hurt in Somara's eyes.

It was cold and the windows of the car were all fogged up since I had turned off the ignition and sat there another fifteen minutes. Finally I walked up the steps and put my key into the lock of the door. I had only stepped three feet into the foyer of the house when Somara opened the double class doors that lead into the living room. There she was standing looking her usual fine, sexy self, but her eyes were swollen and red.

I asked her if David was okay. She ignored my question and asked her own question. "Why are you here? I packed enough clothes for you for at least a week. You walked right by them when you came through the door. We can agree on a day and time for you to pick up the rest of your things when I'm not home. Your briefcase is in your office. I'll go get it."

Softly, I asked her again if David was okay. The second time I asked, she answered me. "His arm is in a cast but he's okay." I told her that I needed to talk to my son.

Her words were quick and harsh. "Talk to him, to tell him what Malcolm? Why his daddy isn't going to be living with him anymore. Be sure to tell him that his daddy has another girlfriend and a baby on the way."

She stood there looking at me with her bottom lip quivering. She was determined not to cry and undoubtedly wanted to say more. Instead she walked away as her voice broke when she said, "He's in his room and he's probably asleep by now."

Somara and I had broken up. Something I never thought would happen to us. I walked upstairs to David's room feeling like a stranger in my own home. Somara was right he was asleep. I sat down on his bed next to him. The cast on his arm was blue, his favorite color. I took the black marker off the nightstand next to his bed to sign his cast. I wrote, *You'll always be Daddy's little man.*

I know he was asleep, but I still kissed him and told him how much I loved him, and that I would always be there whenever he needed me. I knew that Somara wouldn't keep me from seeing him or being a part of his life. Looking around his room at all of his toys, his football that he loved trying to throw to me, and the stick people drawings that hung on his wall, brought back so many memories.

I went downstairs and Somara was standing there in the living room doorway. This time she was holding my briefcase. I wanted to apologize to her for having put her in the position to ask me to leave our home, and also because I had hurt her so much.

I got out the words, "Baby, I'm so very sorry that I've hurt you. I love you Somara and I will always love you. You are definitely a good woman. I wish we could work things out..." She quickly interrupted me.

"That's not going to happen. We're done! I'll never be able to trust you again. Without trust there is no way our relationship could ever work, and what about Ava? You're just going to walk away from her now? You won't be able to do that and I guess that you shouldn't." Her words hurt me then and they still hurt me now. Sometimes when I'm asleep at night, I wake up because I can hear her voice in my ear saying those very words.

Hearing Somara say the words, "We're done" made me feel like I had been stabbed in the heart. What else could she say? I was the one who had ruined things. I was to blame all by myself. Before I left, I told her that I wanted to see David on a regular basis and that I would always take care of him. Those words sounded so final. In the back of my mind, I hoped we could still be together somewhere down the road.

Her voice was softer when she said to me; "You can see David whenever you want. I don't doubt at all that you'll take care of him. You're a good man and you have a good heart. To be honest, you've been good to me. But you know as well as I do, everything that looks good to you, is not good for you. When you have something good, don't gamble with what you're not willing to lose." She was right and she had told me that same thing when we first started dating.

I told her that I would be back on Thursday to pick up the rest of my things and for her not to hesitate to ever call me if she needed anything. To my surprise, she let me kiss her on the cheek. I left feeling very empty inside.

I didn't go back over to Ava's that night, I checked into a hotel that I didn't do much sleeping in at all. Tossing and turning, watching TV, tossing and turning was pretty much what my night consisted of. By the time I got out of the bed, I was just as tired as I was when I had gotten into it.

The next morning, I went over to Ava's. I spent half the day there with her. When I was about to leave she asked me if what Somara said about my spending time in prison was true. I told her that I did serve time on a drug charge. She asked me why I didn't tell her and that opened up a conversation that I really didn't want to get into.

Without thinking I answered her very frankly. "I didn't tell you because we didn't start out with a relationship being our objective. You were my client remember? There are a lot of things that you don't know about me, but Somara does. We have a history together. I shared my life with her, not just my bed." Ava shot back sarcastically, "Thanks for the clarification Malcolm. I get it."

I wanted to take back the harsh words I had said to Ava. They were true but my delivery of the facts was less than sensitive. I apologized to her and tried to smooth things over before I left. When I walked out of the door, Ava still wasn't too happy with me.

Thursday came faster than I wanted it to. I went home to pick up the rest of my things. Or should I say, I went over to Somara's to pick up the rest of my things. It was definitely going to take me awhile to not think of that house as home. Surprisingly, I wasn't bitter about Somara keeping the house. She had more than earned it.

I was taking a load of things out of the small U-Haul trailer that I rented and hitched to the back of my SUV. I had too much stuff to try to fit it all into my Mercedes. But then who moves in a Mercedes? Somara pulled into the driveway. I planned to be gone before she got home. She was early, and I couldn't have planned for that.

Somara said, "Hello" in a tone void of emotion as she walked up the steps to the front door of the house. I loaded the next couple of boxes that were sitting on the ground by the U-Haul. Somara had taken the mail out of the mailbox. Envelopes were laying on the porch at her feet while she held one envelope in her hand and what looked like a piece of clothing. She was just standing there in a daze. I called out to her but she didn't say anything and she didn't move.

I ran up the steps and before I even reached her, the look in her eyes scared me. I asked her what was wrong. She said, "He kept them. This is not going to end. He's not going to

223

leave me alone." I took the garment she had in her hand and the envelope. There was no return address on it.

The envelope had held a pair of black, thigh high cut, size six panties. The note inside read, *"You sure tasted good!"* The police never found the panties that Somara was wearing the night she was raped. Money must have kept them. Somara was shaking; I took her into the house. We talked for at least thirty minutes and I finally got her calmed down. I offered to spend the night. She said that wasn't necessary, she'd be okay.

I took the envelope and the panties and I promised Somara that I wouldn't let anything happen to her. She hugged me tightly and relaxed the weight of her body into my chest for just a few minutes. The same way she had done so many times before. It felt so good, though it was temporary, and that was my fault.

Chapter 27

I spent another night in a hotel, which was something I figured I would be doing until I had time to rent a condo or buy another house. I hadn't even gotten undressed after checking into the hotel. I was tired physically and emotionally. I fell across the bed with my head hanging half way off the side of it, staring at the floor until sleep finally took over.

I could hear a phone ringing far off in the distance. Every time I got up to look for the phone to answer it, I couldn't find it and the phone would stop ringing.

The vibrating pager clipped to my belt woke me up. I looked around the room and realized where I was. My cell phone was ringing too. As I reached for it, I looked at the pager and it was a 911 page. I flipped open my cell phone and answered it. It was Ava and she was in labor. She said she was feeling a lot of pressure in her lower abdomen and back. She had been trying to call me, which meant the ringing phone wasn't all a dream. I told her I was on my way and drove across town as fast I could without getting a speeding ticket.

When I got to Ava's house she was breathing heavily and having a lot of pain in her back, along with sharp pains at the bottom of her stomach. I thought for sure she must have been in hard labor. When I tried to help her up out of the bed, she screamed out in pain. I grabbed the phone and called her doctor. His answering service said he was already at the hospital delivering a baby and for me to get Ava there as quickly as possible.

I picked Ava up and took her out to the car. On the drive to the hospital her pain got worse. She was clinching my hand, breathing hard, and screamed out a couple of times saying the pain was terrible. We were about four blocks from the hospital; I looked over and saw the red blood running down her legs. I remember so clearly her shaky voice saying to me, "Oh my God, I'm bleeding."

I told her to look at me. Not to look at anything else. Just look at me and breathe as slowly as she could. I pulled up to the hospital, Little Company of Mary, blowing my horn as hard as I could. The security guard stepped out of the door and I yelled to him that we needed a doctor right away, because I had a pregnant woman in the car and she was bleeding.

A nurse met us at the car with a wheelchair. The nurse asked me who her doctor was as she hurried through the emergency room doors pushing Somara's wheelchair. We got upstairs on the eighth floor; Ava was quickly put in a birthing room. I was asked to wait outside until Ava could be undressed and the nurse could see how far she had dilated. It wasn't too long before the nurse came out and told me I could go on in and that Ava was fully dilated and in hard labor.

Not even five minutes later the doctor was in the room, the bed had been broken down to a birthing table, and I couldn't remember anything I had learned in Lamaze class. Ava was sweating a lot and her pain seemed to continue to get worse. She was hooked up to a monitor that was spitting out small long sheets of paper with a lot of squiggly lines on it. Two other nurses came into the room.

Dr. Chase told Ava to start pushing. She kept telling me that it hurt too badly and she was too tired to push. As soon as she finished her sentence she had a contraction and screamed out. I helped her exhale through the contraction and push at the same time. That went on for about five minutes. She had one more contraction, pushed hard, and the baby was out.

The baby didn't cry, not even after the doctor took his little body and slapped him on his bottom. Ava was exhausted and breathing heavier than she was before she delivered the baby. A nurse gave her oxygen and said her blood pressure was too high. They would be giving her a shot to bring it down quickly.

I was trying to see what the doctor and the other two people helping him were doing. I still hadn't heard the baby cry, which made me think something had to be wrong. When Dr. Chase turned to me, I was looking straight into his eyes. They told me what his lips were about to say. Before I actually heard the words, I already knew the baby was dead.

The doctor said there was no way to tell that the baby would be still born. Ava was in hard labor when we got to the hospital. Her heart rate was racing, but because the baby's heart rate wasn't immediately detected, Dr. Chase wanted to deliver the baby right away. Not that he had much choice since the baby's head was crowning when he came into the room.

The babies heart must have stopped in the last day or two because Ava had only stopped feeling the baby bouncing around and keeping her up all night for the last couple of days. The placenta and umbilical cord were both very dark and hard. Dr. Chase said the baby's blood flow, oxygen, and nutrients must have been cut off within the last couple of days before Ava gave birth.

She was sleeping and I wasn't going to wake her up. I couldn't imagine what I would say to her, so I sat there trying to deal with my own feelings of loss. I watched Ava sleep, while I really looked past her lying there still and quiet. I saw all the wonderful days and nights that Somara and I had spent together. Our first vacation to Aruba and all the beautiful places that followed. I saw her addictive smile and the sexy way that red dress fit her the first time I met her. I looked over the years that we had been together. Then I saw where we had ended up.

Ava walked into my office and said she needed help with her restaurant. That was the beginning of the end for me. I wasn't blaming her! It was my fault that I had cheated on Somara, and stepped so far away from the man my mother had raised me to be.

Ava was looking at me. I hadn't realized she was awake. She smiled and it was like her face lit up. Reaching her hand out to me, she asked where the baby was. I got up from the chair and sat down next to her on the bed. Then I leaned my body over hers and whispered in her ear, "Our son didn't make it."

I couldn't stand to hear the words said loudly. Ava gasped and wrapped her arms around my upper body and started to cry. She was inconsolable.

The doctor had to give her a sedative. I asked him if she would be able to still have children. He said, "Yes." She needed to wait awhile and let her body heal. But she would be fine. I took solace in that because I hoped one day she would find the man she could share her life with and have children with because I couldn't be that man. I kissed her gently knowing that it would be for the last time.

I sat with Ava until I was sure that she was resting comfortably. I took a few minutes and wrote her a quick note.

Ava,

I feel bad about allowing you into my life without really being free to do that. It was wrong of me, and for that, I'm sorry. You are a beautiful woman and you deserve more than I can give you. I do, however, want you to know that what I felt for you was more than just concern because you were pregnant with my child. My heart had grown to love you!

Malcolm

Chapter 28

I sat across the street in my car. It had to be his house. At least it was the address on the letter he sent Somara. I thought about what was next, briefly wondering if there was any way the outcome could be different. The fact that I had been betrayed by someone who I brought up out of the trenches, lives had been forever changed, and a shadow of fear was determined to not let go of its victim, were the reasons why I couldn't change the course I was on.

The streetlights were on but not within a block or two of the house. Maybe the kids in the neighborhood had used them for target practice with their BB guns. I sat in the dark for about two hours. All the lights in the house that I had been watching finally went out. A tall bulky image walked out of the door and turned around to lock it. The rage inside of me stood up straight. I put my hand on the door handle of my car. I counted his steps as he walked across the street to his BMW that was sitting a couple of cars away in front of mine. When he reached for his car door, I stepped out of mine quietly. The next thing he heard was the sound of my voice.

"Put your hands on top of the car, right now. Lean your body in against the door of the car."

He knew exactly who was talking to him. His voice had a strong arrogant tone. "Malcolm, What's up man? We on opposite sides of the fence?"

There was no turning back and I was strong in my convictions when I answered, "We've been on opposite sides of the fence for some time now, and you put us there. Don't play games with me. You know what this is about."

I didn't hear any fear in his voice when he replied, "If you mean that fine woman of yours, you can't be upset because a man wants to see his son."

I've played that encounter with him, over and over in my mind. That's why I can remember it so clearly. I can hear myself saying to him, "I wouldn't be mad at you if you were the kind of man that had his son with a woman the right way. But you're not a man, you're an animal."

Even when he was at the threshold of something ugly and final, he was still arrogant and full of himself when he said, "You know how we do it man. We take what we want."

I told him, "A woman's dignity is not something that you take." Then I tossed the panties he had mailed to Somara on top of his car.

He leaned his face in toward the panties and said, "They still smell like her sweet juices."

I was tired of hearing the sound of his voice. The last thing I said to him was, "Remember that sweet smell where you're going. Unlike you, who rapes women from behind, I want you to see it coming. Step backwards away from the car and turn around."

It was then that he could see the steel cold nine-millimeter gun I was holding. Finally, there it was in his eyes, what looked to me like fear. He started to say something as he reached for the gun that I was sure that he had in his jacket. I cut his words off with a single shot to his forehead. It took a couple of seconds before his body fell to the ground. I looked into his eyes as he went down.

Money, a brother I brought along with me on my ride to the top. No one in my circle came closer to me trusting them than him. He set me up with the Fed's and even tried to pin a murder for hire charge on me. Then he raped my woman and gave her the child that should have been mine. He was a sorry, worthless, maggot of a man with no honor. I couldn't look the other way. Not that time. The iron doors closed shut behind me. An orange jumpsuit and a cell that I shared with another man welcomed me back to penitentiary life.

This time I'm serving a thirty-year prison sentence for murder. There was no colorful spin put on my defense. I plead guilty to first-degree murder. I had given it a lot of thought. The decision wasn't hard. He had to die. But I had some honor. I looked him in the face, eye to eye, before I took his life. Now when I close my eyes at night in my cold, dark cell, it's his face that I see. I'm looking down at him, lying in a casket.

I pray that you will enjoy the sneak preview of my next book:

The Kitchen Beautician

It is a hilariously colorful look at life and the decisions that people make and how those decisions impact their lives. As the story unfolds you will find an unexpected love story that will melt your heart.

Chapter 1

You met the "Kitchen Beautician" Javon, in my first book "Where The Brothers At?" In case you didn't read the book, allow me to introduce you to Javon. He's the handsome gay brother that owns a lively neighborhood beauty shop. It's a shop that's also the hang out for those who want to hear all the juicy gossip and get the best advice in town, while they get their hair laid to the max.

Women stood in awe of the beautiful specimen of a man, Javon. He was six feet tall, with six-pack abs that rippled down the front of his shirt. They even wanted to rest theirs heads on his chest and biceps, while grabbing a hand full of his fine, firm butt cheeks. His perfectly groomed mustache looked so good lying against his smooth dark brown skin. Between Javon's million-dollar smile and soft, luscious, short, darks curls, it was hard not to do a double take when you looked at him.

Entering Javon's beauty shop was like stepping into your mama's living room. The one room in the house where only company was allowed; that was the room where mama kept the very best things she owned on display. Javon's beauty shop was no different.

The walls were strategically covered with art by many of the Black artist Javon admired the most. His favorite piece entitled "Embrace" by Edward Clay Wright, hung on the wall just above Javon's styling chair. The captivating image of a beautiful Nubian woman wrapped in the embrace of a man caressing her so passionately that their love was felt by anyone who merely glanced at the exquisite painting. It made just the statement of elegance Javon wanted everyone to see when they entered his beauty shop.

The plush leather chair that seated everyone, as Javon made them into his newest masterpiece, also had a hidden foot sauna, which could be made visible with the push of a button. Just in case someone wanted to get a pedicure while they got their hair sculpted. The theme of "head to toe" pampering was in full affect.

The stunning granite champagne bar at the far end of the room would quickly draw anyone's attention. It was stocked with alcoholic and non-alcoholic beverages. Fresh baked homemade pastries, fresh cut fruit, and even an attractive hand dipped selection of chocolate fruits and nuts were deliciously displayed at the end of the champagne bar.

The hidden foot sauna wasn't the only spectacular feature that made the chair, which sat directly in the middle of Javon's shop, an undeniable conversation piece. Italian imported black leather covered the genuine gold frame, which had twelve different settings that delivered a relaxing and therapeutic massage.

The chair even had the hydraulics of a low rider. Javon could press, perm, curl, cremp or braid hair at any angle with just the touch of a foot pedal. The foot pedal allowed him the rotational versatility he wanted, without having to constantly tilt the person's head back and forth, to get the angle he needed to repair any nappy kitchen.

Behind him stood a midnight black workstation that held the "top of the line" hair styling equipment. Each piece of equipment, from the brush to the Marcel curling iron, was black and gold toned. Javon believed in sculpting each individual masterpiece in style.

Here's where the story begins. Kesha, one of Javon's faithful and long time customers was almost running late for her hair appointment. She called Javon to let him know that she would be there shortly. Between her regular workouts at the gym and her commitment to eating healthy, Kesha had a body that said, "Ooh wee, I'm working it."

Her successful catering business provided the funds for her to live a very comfortable life style. However, Kesha, like a lot of folks didn't always make the best decisions. Because of that, she was about to get a mouthful of advice that would make her head spin, and give her a few things to consider.

"Hey Javon! This is Kesha. I'm running a little late for my hair appointment. Don't fill my spot in the chair."

"Girlfriend, you know the rules. You've got ten minutes. If you're not step'n through my door within ten minutes of your appointment time, somebody else will be sitt'n down in my chair."

"Okay, I'll be turning down your street in just a second. I've still got six minutes. I can make it," pleaded Kesha.

Javon let out a long sigh and said, "Alright, we'll see. My Marcel curling iron is spitting sparks right now. See you in a few."

"Javon, you almost done with me?"

"Relax Gladys. Perfection can't be rushed! A couple of extra minutes won't hurt this mane of yours!"

"Ooh," rumbled the women sitting in the front of the shop. "Javon, you know you are too real," said the woman who was next in line to sit in Javon's chair if Kesha didn't walk through the door quickly.

"You got that right and that's why ya'll love me! Ya'll front like you love coming here to get your hair done. It's true you come here to get your short hair weaved down to your butt, your course hair permed, and some of you still think you look good in those ridiculous doo doo braids. With my skills, I manage to implant micro braids on heads of hair so short; I can smell the nasty thoughts still lingering in your head from the bedroom beat down, that you gave somebody else's husband the night before. Yeah, I'm the coldest hair doing diva around. No doubt!"

"But the real reason you come up in here is to hear my for real, straight talk, curling iron counseling, which for some of you is just me saying what you already know and don't want to accept. Most of you act like unless you hear the cold hard truth delivered with precision from my nickel-plated magnum mouth; you would have never considered some of the advice I give. Often times it's that same advice that keeps you from spiraling downward into an abyss of bad relationship and life decisions."

"Some of you act like you're afraid of life and you need somebody's stamp of approval. Especially when you know you've totally screwed up and the poor choices you've made are staring you in the face because now you have to live with the consequences of those poor choices everyday."

The salon filled with laughter as Gladys, who was just getting up from Javon's chair said, "Ya'll know he telling the truth, because most of you keep some type of drama going on all the time."

Javon took a bow and said, "I love ya'll too." Kesha rushed in and slide into Javon's chair so quick the seat was still warm from Gladys's boat size rump shaker. She made her appointment with no time to spare. Kesha knew Javon didn't play when it came to folks being late for an appointment in his chair.

Kesha saluted everybody in the shop with a cheerful "What's up ya'll?" The responses to her greeting were just as lively.

Along with a few women throwing her compliments about her hot Juicy Couture outfit.

"Javon, I told you I would make it on time. Here I am, now work your magic." Kesha took her hat off and, along with her hat, off came her wig.

"I'll have to work overtime on this matted mess you call hair. Girl, just because you wear a wig, doesn't mean you don't have to comb your hair underneath it." The laughter that bellowed through the shop could have shaken the windows. Kesha slid down in Javon's chair a couple of inches as she put her wig and hat into her purse.

"So what's happening with you Kesha?" Javon asked as he dug the comb down into Kesha's matted mess of a head.

"Well… I got a man!"

"Oh no, not celibate Sally," Javon said when he heard the news.

"Shut up Javon. Yes, I'm celibate, but I can still get a man."

"Yeah, right! He must be in a wheel chair or in prison if he's willing to not get any of the good stuff."

Kesha sucked in her lips, looked up at the ceiling, then turned and looked up at Javon and smiled without showing any teeth. "He ah ... he ah. Javon stopped her right there. Her nervous response gave it away.

"Girl you got to be kid'n. A jail bird, please! Help us Lord! How did you meet him?"

"My friend Jonita's man is in the same prison. His cousin, James, wanted a pen pal. So I started writing to him. About three months later I rode down to the prison in Danville Illinois with Jonita to visit. She saw her man and I met James. The brother is too fine! About six feet tall and his arms are as big as cannons."

"That's what the prison yard workout does for the biceps. What else do you think he has time to do?"

"Dang Javon, stop hate'n. He's fine, smart, and he's not on the left side of sweet. You just jealous and wish you had him."

"Honey please! He can't be too smart, he in prison."

"He's an accountant. His partner embezzled money from some of their largest clients. James was innocent. He just got caught up in something that his partner was guilty of."

Quiet laughter rumbled through the shop. Several customers let down the lids on their hair dryers and went back to singeing their curls dry after they had gotten an ear full. But they let the lids on the dryers down too soon. Javon had a couple more things to say.

"You know what, you're right. He is smart if he got you coming down to see him and no doubt spending money on him too, right?"

"I've done a few things to help him. He is my man."

Janese snickered and said, "Your man?" in a questioning tone. Janese was a first time visitor to the shop. Javon looked over at her and said, "Don't worry honey, I got this."

"Girl please, tell the whole story. If he's anything like the last prison man you dated, I know how this will all turn out. What was his name? Del Ray, Del Rose, something like that."

"His name was DeLantae, thank you!"

"Now, you know I love you and you also know I'm gonna tell you like it is. You're an intelligent woman, but sometimes you act like you and common sense don't know each other. Between paying DeLantae's child support, sending money to help pay rent for some woman he told you was his sister, but ended up being his other girlfriend, and all the money you put on his books, I thought you would have learned a few things."

It was like watching a fifty-two inch TV screen with surround sound. All eyes were on Kesha and Javon. A couple of people's cell phones rang and were immediately silenced. It appeared that nobody wanted to miss a word that was said.

"Yeah, I know Javon. He wasn't who I thought he was. But this guy is different."

"Come on Kesha. He's a Prison Pimp. Just like DeLantae was. Pimps take from you and use you. That's exactly what he's doing to you. James doesn't give you anything. You're the one doing all the giving and he's calling the shots and doing all the taking. Come visit me, write me, accept my collect phone calls, and put money on my books. That's all you're hearing from him. If you weren't celibate, he couldn't even give you any. Why? Because he's locked up!"

"I know, I know, Javon. My mama told me the same thing."

"That's right girl, you don't need him. You deserve better," chimed in the two ladies that were talking about a similar experience.

"Kesha, don't misunderstand me. I'm not saying there aren't some good guys that happen to be in prison. Hell, there are some innocent good guys in prison. I'm just telling you there are some better places to consider meeting a man than the prison gates. There's a brother out there just for you."

"Why it gotta be a brother Javon? It's some fine White boys out there and I dated an Italian that made my knees buckle every time he kissed me."

"Kesha you need to read the book "Where The Brothers At?" One of the things it deals with is interracial relationships. I'm telling you girl, the book was hot." Trish promised as she licked her lips and shook her right hand back and forth to help her nails dry faster.

"What ever works for you, Kesha, that's what you go with. The color of his skin doesn't matter; it's about what's in his heart. The color of his skin can't love you, but his heart can. Whoever you date, make sure he brings something to the relationship and the relationship should enhance who you are as a person. Don't look for the relationship to define you. A man wants a woman that's happy with herself and confident about who she is in her own right. Men don't like clingy insecure women."

Trish was quick to agree. "You're definitely right Javon. My brother says the same thing all the time about his girlfriend. She too darn clingy and he can't stand it. You think Kesha is in a crazy relationship; I'm in love with a married man."

Javon instantly stopped pulling the comb through Kesha's hair. He stepped from behind the styling chair Kesha was sitting in and with his eyes sternly focused on Trish he said, "Girlfriend, girlfriend, hold up. Wait a minute! You dating a married man, somebody else's husband." Then he asked, "How many women in here are married?"

The conversation from there gets hot and heavy. To find out what Javon has to say about the other woman (women dating married men), brothers on the down low, and several other situations his customers find themselves in and the consequences of the decisions they make, watch for the November 2009 release of *"The Kitchen Beautician."*

Thank you for reading *"Sorrows of the Heart"* and I hope you enjoyed the sneak preview of my third book,

"*The Kitchen Beautician*." I appreciate your support tremendously and I pray that God's grace and mercy will be ever abounding in your life.

Gracie Hill

LaVergne, TN USA
10 November 2010
204328LV00001BA/5/P